SUCCESS!

Kiki thanked Mrs. Kendrick twice and hung up, then grabbed Pumpkin and danced him around the kitchen. "Perfect! Perfect! Perfect!" she chanted to the astonished cat. Kiki rushed back over to the phone and dialed Andrew's number. "You won't believe it!" she said when he picked up the phone. "I got an internship, too! Elena and I will both be toiling in the halls of the Galliard Museum next week!"

Berkley/Splash Books by Louise Munro Foley

"THIEF!" SAID THE CAT
"BLOOD!" SAID THE CAT

"POISON" SAID THE CAT
(September 1992)

"BLOOD!"
SAID THE CAT

Louise
Munro Foley

SPLASH™

A BERKLEY / SPLASH BOOK

Dedicated with love to my mother,
Mary R. Munro,
who has a thing about cats . . .

Chapter One

Fourteen-year-old Kiki Collier swung open the passenger door and climbed out onto the curving driveway in front of the Galliard Museum of Fine Arts.

"Thanks for the lift, Mom. Does this look okay?" she asked as she retucked her blouse inside the waistband of her skirt.

"You look wonderful. Very professional." Dr. Maryanne Collier smiled at her lanky, red-haired daughter as Kiki inspected her nylons and medium-heeled pumps. "It's not often I see you all dressed up on a Saturday!"

"It's not often I have to interview the curator of a museum," said Kiki. "Not exactly regular stuff for the Pioneer Junior High *Courier*! Elena would eat this up, but I really feel weird. Why did she have to pick today to get sick?"

Elena Morgan was another student reporter for *The Courier*. She usually covered art

1

news for the paper—ballet, the Glee Club's annual operetta, and the drama society's productions.

"Well, Andrew knew you'd do a good job on it. He wouldn't have called you this morning if he didn't think so."

"He just didn't want to do it himself," Kiki grumbled good-naturedly. "Some friend! When you've got a staff of three and one's sick and the second is the editor . . . guess who gets the assignment?"

"I know you'll do just fine," said Dr. Collier, looking at her watch. "I've got to run. I'm due at the hospital at one. See you about nine-thirty tonight. Got your notebook?"

Kiki reached to the floor of the backseat to pull a notebook from her backpack, and let out a wail. "Mom! How did Pumpkin get in the car?"

Sitting primly behind the backpack, quiet as a sphinx, was a huge orange cat who gazed innocently up at Kiki through alert and loving green eyes.

"I can't take you in there!" She looked toward the imposing stone building with its ivy-covered walls. "Pumpkin! You're—you're—" As she struggled to find the word, the cat climbed out of the car and, with great dignity, repositioned himself on the sidewalk beside her. "Mom! I can't take him to the interview!"

"Sorry, Kiki," said Dr. Collier firmly. "I don't have to time take him home." Her voice softened. "It's not like it's the first time this has happened, honey. And it looks like he's on his best behavior."

As if he was acknowledging the compliment, the large cat swished his bushy tail around to encircle his front feet.

"Do you have bus fare to get home?"

"Yes."

"Do you have your backpack?"

Kiki nodded and reached in to get the bag.

"I guess you'll have to put him in the bag and hope for the best. I've really got to go. Good luck with the interview!" She shifted the car into gear and pulled out of the driveway. Kiki let out a slow sigh and stared at the cat sitting like a marble sculpture in front of her.

"You are a bad cat!" she said, trying to sound convincing. Her mother was right. It was not the first time Pumpkin had pulled this trick. He often got out and followed her to school or the store. In the fall, he had even followed her to a babysitting job, and the house was broken into. She had been glad he was around when he helped chase off the burglars. "You're logging more time in this backpack than my books!" she told him.

Moving with studied calm, the cat walked into the blue denim bag and made himself comfortable.

"I guess I'll have to carry my notebook," Kiki mumbled to herself. "I don't dare reach in there once I get into the museum. I know you too well to give you that opportunity!" An obedient meow came from the depths of the interior.

She hoisted the bag to her shoulder and walked up the wide steps leading to the entrance of the museum. Several people were looking at sculptures in one of the three large exhibit rooms that opened off the marble-floored rotunda. Kiki stopped and looked around for offices.

"May I help you, miss?"

A gray-haired woman wearing a gray skirt, navy blazer, and white blouse approached from a desk in the foyer.

"I'm looking for Mr. Van Kayser's office," Kiki said. "He's expecting me."

"Dr. Van Kayser's office is on the third floor," the woman said, gently stressing the title. She pointed up, and Kiki's eyes followed her gesture.

Arching skyward, the elegantly decorated

4

domed roof of the museum was visible from the circular foyer, giving visitors at the main entrance a view of all three floors. A railing of wrought iron circled a balcony on each floor, and Kiki could see openings to other exhibit rooms, softly illuminated with indirect lighting. A wide, gently curving marble staircase led to the second floor.

"Take the elevator and turn right. His door is marked."

"Thank you," said Kiki, moving toward the elevators.

"Oh, miss! You can leave your backpack in the cloakroom."

Kiki turned. "I'll be needing it," she stammered. "For the interview. I need my . . ." She was going to say *notebook*, until she glanced at the one so obviously clutched in her hand. She looked guiltily at the woman.

"Camera?" asked the woman, looking pleased with herself that she had guessed the contents.

Without replying, Kiki returned her smile and stepped into the elevator. Pumpkin shifted in the bag as they slowly ascended. "Cool it back there!" she whispered, reaching around and patting the bag. "You're a camera."

She got off the elevator and walked to the right, past several unmarked, closed doors. At the end of the hall was a door with a frosted glass pane on which *Ludwig Van Kayser, Curator*, was stenciled in black and gold letters.

As she approached Kiki could hear angry voices—an argument was in progress in the curator's office. She stopped at the door, unsure of what she should do. Knock and interrupt? Walk back to the elevator and approach the door again? Or stand and listen?

"No one will believe you!" a man shouted. "One more innuendo like that and I'll fire you!"

"You wouldn't dare!" said a woman's accented voice.

A hiss seeped out of the bag on Kiki's back.

"Mind your own business, Pumpkin!" Kiki whispered sternly. "This isn't your argument!" But despite her warning, the bag lurched and was suddenly limp as the big cat leaped from its interior and flung himself into the closed door with a thump and a chilling shriek.

The voices stopped and the door opened quickly to reveal a tall, dark-haired man wearing an expensive black three-piece suit, and a short, wiry older woman in dusty blue coveralls and thick glasses. Stunned by their sudden appearance, Kiki stared, and then grabbed for Pumpkin. But she was too late.

The orange cat snarled and jumped at the man, causing him to stagger back into the office.

"Oh! I'm sorry," she apologized, moving to grasp the hissing cat. But the woman in coveralls was faster. She snatched Pumpkin into her arms and stalked off down the hall with a triumphant toss of her head, making a noise that sounded very much like that of the hissing cat.

The man's pale blue eyes narrowed as he watched the woman stride down the hall. The sequence of events happened so fast that Kiki just stood there, immobile and silent, as the woman disappeared around the corner, Pumpkin with her.

"Miss Morgan?" the man asked, catching her arm.

"Yes . . . uh, no, Collier," she replied.

His look of anger was now replaced by a less-genuine smiling mask, and his voice was smooth and welcoming, betraying no hint of the shouting match Kiki had overheard.

"You're from the junior-high newspaper?" Without waiting for her to answer, he went on, "Come in, please!"

"The cat . . ." said Kiki in a weak voice, still looking down the hallway.

"Mrs. Janssen thinks we're running a zoo

7

instead of a museum," the man said, drawing Kiki into the office and closing the door. "She is forever coming to work with some creature in tow. The restoration studio is like a menagerie. Although I must say, I haven't seen that one before. . . . Here! Come and sit over here in this comfortable chair."

In a courtly European fashion, he took her elbow and firmly guided her toward a chair. Kiki quickly assessed the situation. Pumpkin would be safe with an animal lover who worked in the restoration lab of the museum. *Get the interview, keep your mouth shut about cat ownership, and pick Pumpkin up on the way out,* she counseled herself.

She turned her attention to Dr. Van Kayser, who was sitting in the chair opposite hers. Between them, at knee level, was a circular coffee table, its rich, dark wood surface inlaid with a design in mother-of-pearl. The office was elegantly appointed with a thick carpet, heavy draperies, and antique furniture, and natural light filtered down from a skylight above. A pair of large brass urns flanked the door, and the shelves that lined the mahogany-paneled walls held curios which all looked rare and valuable.

"Elena Morgan wasn't feeling well today," Kiki explained to the distinguished-looking man whose cold eyes negated his smile. "So I was asked to come in her place. I'm Kiki Collier."

"It's a pleasure to meet you, Miss Collier," he said, reaching for her hand. Although his manicured nails suggested softness, Kiki noticed that his grip was firm. "I am Ludwig Van Kayser. I will give you my card so you will have the correct spelling," he continued, handing her an embossed ivory-colored card. "What is the thrust of your article?"

Kiki had the uncomfortable feeling that Dr. Van Kayser knew more about interviewing than she did. Her experience to date had been confined to school staff members—the baseball coach, the school nurse, one of the custodians—with whom she felt comfortable. Dr. Van Kayser did not fit into that category and, his pleasant demeanor aside, there was something about the man that she didn't like. The feeling mirrored Pumpkin's reaction, and Pumpkin was hardly ever wrong about people.

"*The Courier* is doing a series of articles on careers," she explained, "to give the students a broader view of employment opportunities. In your case, we're taking a look behind the scenes in the arts world."

Dr. Van Kayser leaned back and stared beyond her, smiling as though enjoying a private joke. "The field is very limited for employment opportunities, of course," he began, his snobbish tone making it clear that only an exceptional few could hope to attain a position such as his. Kiki took notes as he talked about educational requirements—a doctorate in fine arts, an apprenticeship at a recognized museum, years of experience in recognizing art objects of true value—and the need for an unshakeable passion for antiquities that left little time for a personal life.

True value . . . Kiki said to herself, suddenly recalling a newspaper clipping she'd looked at that morning from the file Andrew had dropped off. "I'd like to go back to your comment on genuine articles as opposed to forgeries," she said, interrupting the curator's monologue. She knew she was wandering away from the assigned topic. But now that she'd thought of it, something about the story she had read bothered her, aside from the bad vibes she was getting from Dr. Van Kayser. Kiki chose her words carefully. "Recently there was an article in the paper about something in the Galliard Museum that turned out to be a fake. How does something like that happen when museum personnel are so highly trained and the evaluation precautions you mentioned are used?"

His smile faded somewhat. "Yes," he said. "A vase in the Greek collection, acquired before I came, I believe. I was in London on a buying trip when it was discovered. Fortunately, such instances occur rarely. Unfortunately, the press, even at a minor level"—he stared at her coldly—"likes to highlight the sensational." His sarcastic remark made it clear to Kiki that she had stumbled into forbidden territory.

She frowned, thinking of the newspaper clipping, and decided to continue her line of questioning despite Dr. Van Kayser's comments. "The article said the forgery was spotted by an employee. What position would that person hold?"

Dr. Van Kayser paused before answering. "I believe it was the person from the restoration lab," he replied. "Had I been here, the article in question would never have reached the display area. It was a crude copy. Quite identifiable as fraudulent, even by an amateur!" He gestured with his hand to indicate that the incident was not worth further discussion, but more questions were forming in Kiki's mind.

"Who else on the staff besides yourself and the restorer would have the knowledge to spot a fake?" she asked, remembering the argument she had heard from the hall.

"Miss Collier, this is a small museum with a fine collection. I am the only knowledgeable expert at the Galliard. There is no assistant curator, there is no appraiser on staff. We call in outside consultants when there is a need. The appraiser who assessed that particular piece is no longer on the Galliard's list of approved contractors. Our funds are expended on acquiring objects and not on personnel."

Kiki rested her notebook on her lap and doggedly continued asking questions. "You talked about a restoration lab, or studio," she said. "What are the qualifications for that kind of position? How many people work there? Wouldn't a restorer have to know a lot about the arts, too?"

An expression of impatience crossed the curator's face. "Restorers are necessary for large institutions that enjoy unlimited funding and have constantly changing exhibitions. Our restoration studio is staffed, at the present, by one minimally qualified employee who was hired on a sympathy vote by some members of the Board of Trustees—most of whom, by the way, are amateur collectors or dilettantes. I opposed retaining the studio here at all, on the grounds that our acquisitions should be restricted to items in mint condition. However, I was overruled." He stood up. "And now, if you'll excuse me, I have some important calls to make." He flashed the same plastic public-relations smile he had given her on her arrival and smoothly ushered her out the door.

Kiki stood in the hall for a moment, thinking. She had touched a nerve, or the curator would not have been so defensive. Her intuition, which Andrew said always got her into trouble, told her that there was something strange going on at the Galliard Museum. Dr. Van Kayser never had answered her question about the qualifications needed by a restorer. The woman he had been arguing with must have been the employee who spotted the fake. What had he meant about a sympathy vote? Why had they been arguing? What wouldn't people believe?

The investigative reporter in Kiki kicked into high gear. There was a story at this museum, but it wasn't about job possibilities. Dr. Van Kayser had given her plenty of material for a *Courier* article. Now she was going to ferret out the real story! And her next step was to talk to the feisty little woman who had snatched up Pumpkin before he could attack the curator again.

Chapter Two

In the main-floor rotunda, Kiki approached the woman who had directed her to the curator's office a half-hour earlier.

"Where is the restoration studio?" she asked.

"Lower level, miss, but no visitors are allowed down there."

"Dr. Van Kayser said I could interview Mrs., uh, Jensen," Kiki fibbed, fumbling for the name she had heard Dr. Van Kayser use. *Besides*, she thought, *I have to retrieve my cat. But I'm not going to tell you that!*

"Janssen," the woman said, frowning. "Mrs. Janssen. It's very irregular. But I guess if Dr. Van Kayser said so . . . take the stairway at the end of the hall. The studio is on your left."

"Thanks," said Kiki, hurrying away before the woman could change her mind or check the truth of her story.

The basement hallway was dimly lit. A pile of empty packing crates teetered at the foot of the stairway, and a muted but high-pitched whine coming from behind one of the doors grated on Kiki's ears as she turned left. The noise stopped, and was followed by a familiar squeal. Pumpkin! She grinned. This was the place! She rapped on the unmarked door and was rewarded with a thump and a scratching noise from inside. As she put her hand on the knob the door jerked open. The cat jumped at her enthusiastically, and the woman she had seen on the third floor stared at her, unsmiling.

"Yes?" she asked curtly.

Kiki picked up Pumpkin and was treated to an animated, rough-tongued face washing.

"Yes?" the woman repeated. "You wish something?"

"Yes," said Kiki, looking over Mrs. Janssen's shoulder into the room. "I wanted to thank you for keeping my cat for me . . . and I wanted to talk to you for a minute. May I see your studio?"

Mrs. Janssen shrugged and stepped aside, allowing Kiki to enter. She closed the door. "You are welcome," she said in a European accent that made the *w*'s sound like *v*'s. "Your cat, he is amiable." The first hint of softening appeared at the corners of her mouth as she reached up and stroked Pumpkin. "We became friends."

"Pumpkin can tell when a person likes him," Kiki replied.

"I am Gabrielle Janssen," the woman said. And then she added cautiously, "You are a friend of Dr. Van Kayser?"

"No. I just met him today. My name's Kiki Collier. I interviewed him for our school newspaper. We're doing a series on jobs in various fields." She paused, and her gaze wandered around the room. "I've never been in a restoration studio before. May I look around?"

Mrs. Janssen looked relieved. "But of course. Kiki—that is an odd name."

"It's short for Kathryn Kristine."

A workbench along one wall was cluttered with tools and bottles and brushes, and the room smelled of turpentine. A small drill, similar to the one in Kiki's dentist's office, was suspended with its bit end hanging directly over a metal dagger that lay on the bench. "Is that what I heard when I was in the hall?"

"The drill? Yes," said Mrs. Janssen, nodding. "The hours, the minutes, the seconds, eat at the metal. And the environment! The very air we breathe creates cavities in metal, as sugar does in the tooth. The buffer can sometimes smooth the surface, as when your teeth are cleaned." She seized the drill and demonstrated, pointing, as a tiny corrosion disappeared under the whining instrument.

Pumpkin wailed his disapproval, and Mrs. Janssen shut off the drill and smiled at him.

"That's amazing!" said Kiki. "I didn't expect to find a dentist's drill in a museum. Or this—this looks like Marlex!" She picked up a square of fabric that resembled fine netting.

"It is unusual that one so young should know medical supplies," said Mrs. Janssen, looking at her questioningly.

"I don't, really," Kiki said. "But my mother's a doctor and she showed me some of this and explained how surgeons use it to help close a wound. I used it for a science-fair project a couple of years ago."

"Oh, yes. And what will strengthen the flesh will also strengthen old pottery. I use many of the physician's tools." She opened a leather case to expose a set of razor-sharp scalpels and stainless-steel probes.

"That's cool!" said Kiki.

"Our jobs are not that different," Mrs. Janssen continued. "The surgeon repairs damaged bodies, and I repair damaged artifacts. We who work with ancient treasures find many aids in modern technology." She reached over and stroked Pumpkin, who was nestled in Kiki's arms. "You have a nice cat. Even Monet likes him."

There was a muffled woof from a corner of the long room, and an elderly dog—part basset hound, Kiki thought, judging from his low-slung body and droopy ears—heaved himself up from a blanket on the floor and lumbered over to join them.

With Monet trudging at her heels and Pumpkin still in her arms, Kiki wandered around the large, oblong room, staring first at the antique items shelved against one wall and then at the workbench with its tools and chemicals, and finally at a large, ornately framed oil painting of a pastoral scene that was sitting on its side with padded clamps holding one corner of the frame together.

"Do you fix all these things, Mrs. Janssen?" Kiki asked.

"Gabrielle," the woman corrected. "You must call me Gabrielle. To say Mrs. Janssen makes it seem that you are angry with me. A friend does not call a person so formally." She paused. "Dr. Van Kayser calls me Mrs. Janssen. That is proper. I am not his friend."

"I overheard part of your argument with him. He was very angry."

"He is a scheming, unethical man!" Gabrielle said heatedly. "If he were not here, I would quit!"

Kiki turned and faced her. "I don't understand. If you dislike him so much, wouldn't it be easier to quit and not have to deal with him every day?"

Gabrielle nodded. "Easier, yes. But one pays a high price for taking the easy path through life. Things were different here when my Roland was the curator."

"Your husband?"

"Yes. For thirty-nine years he guided the Galliard collection."

"Have you worked here that long, too?"

"Oh, no! For those years I worked at my home studio, helping Roland when I could. He would bring things home. 'Can you fix it, Gabrielle?' he would ask. An abrasion on a piece of sculpture, a scratch on a canvas, a chipped pot—little things. And then he got sick, and he was sick for a long time. I continued to do little things for the museum—small repairs that needed to be taken care of to maintain the collection. And when Roland died, the Board of Trustees asked me to serve temporarily as acting curator until his successor could be found."

"And his successor was Dr. Van Kayser."

Gabrielle removed her thick-lensed glasses and squinted. "Yes!" she snapped, rubbing the glasses on the front of her coveralls, adding at least as much dust as she was removing. "And when I learned it was he, I could not leave."

"Why?"

"I could not leave a lifetime of my husband's work in the hands of that charlatan! So I pleaded poverty and asked the Board to keep me on as a restorer. It was not exactly a falsehood—Roland's medical bills were very large—although it was not my real reason for wanting to stay." She slipped her glasses back on her nose and smiled ruefully. "So I am now a watchdog to Van Kayser, just as Monet is a watchdog to me." She leaned over and patted the hound, who responded with a satisfied guttural sigh.

"Then you knew Dr. Van Kayser before he came here?"

"I did. I worked with him in Vienna for four years. When I knew him, he was a brash young man with a lot of talent and no discipline. And finally, as with many weak, impatient men, greed corrupted him. Only he was known then as Ludwig Stottmeier."

"You mean he changed his name?"

Gabrielle arched an eyebrow. "Yes."

"Why?"

She hesitated before she spoke. "He caused some embarrassment for one of his employers—a small but respected European institution."

"Didn't you tell the Galliard trustees about it?"

Gabrielle moved to the workbench and began vigorously polishing the dagger with a cloth. "Who would listen to me? They would just say I wanted my Roland back, that I was crazy with grief."

Dr. Van Kayser's angry words replayed in Kiki's head: *No one will believe you!*

"The trustees were not interested in what I had to say. They looked at his paper credentials, his resumé, and they listened to his— how do you say it?—his *line*, his public relations, and they hired him." Her shoulders drooped. "So be it. I am an old woman who talks too much." She looked at Kiki apprehensively. "You are a reporter. But I must ask you not to write about this."

"No, of course not," Kiki assured her.

Pumpkin, bored with all the conversation, wiggled in her arms, and Kiki lowered him to the floor. He walked over to the blanket in the corner and curled up in the spot Monet had vacated.

"You worked at a museum in Vienna?" Kiki asked.

Gabrielle nodded. "Before we came to the United States. After we came here, I stayed home and worked on my own projects."

"Are you an artist?"

"I paint," Gabrielle said. "And I also do some sculpture. And I have a wheel and a kiln."

"A wheel?"

"A potter's wheel."

"I should have been interviewing you!" Kiki said.

"You must come to my place sometime," Gabrielle said. "I would like to show you my things."

"I'd like that, too," said Kiki. She checked her watch. "Right now, I've got to get going or I'll miss my bus."

She picked up an unwilling Pumpkin, put him in the backpack, and shook hands with Gabrielle Janssen. "Thanks," she said on her way out. "I really enjoyed talking with you."

Later that night Kiki went into the living room and sat on the couch beside her mother. She had been bothered all evening with thoughts that Dr. Van Kayser would talk the board into firing Gabrielle. Pumpkin, afraid he was going to be left out of a conversation, crawled out of the copper wash boiler on the hearth that they used to store firewood and plunked himself down at Kiki's feet. "Mom, what do you do if you have a feeling that something is not quite right, but you're not sure what it is?"

Dr. Collier put down her book and tousled her daughter's red curls. "Depends on what it is," she said. "When I'm with a patient, for instance, I usually go with my gut feeling. Something going wrong at school?"

"No. Not at school."

"Well, Kiki, I guess I'd try to find out the whole story."

"Thanks. That's what I thought, too," Kiki said, grinning. She stood up and leaned over to hug her mother. "Good night. See you in the morning."

Dr. Collier gave her a halfhearted smile. "Oh, dear. I think I've just given you permission to do something," she said, "and I'm not sure what."

"Not to worry, Mom."

"That's the last thing I wanted to hear you say! Good night."

Chapter Three

Kiki and Andrew met in the *Courier* office on the second floor of Pioneer Junior High on Monday morning.

"How did it go at the Galliard?" Andrew asked.

"Better than I thought it would," Kiki said. "I think I got more than an interview on employment opportunities in the arts!" She quickly briefed Andrew about her meetings with Dr. Van Kayser and Gabrielle Janssen.

"He's a real scuzzball," Kiki finished, wrinkling her nose. "Even Pumpkin picked up bad vibes from him. I think I'm hot on a *real* story, but I'm not sure what to do about it. I can't think of any plausible way to hang around the place and find out more."

"Kiki, the investigative reporter, rides again!"

"Don't tease, Andrew," said Kiki crossly. She could feel her temper flaring. "You may not trust my sixth sense, but Pumpkin is never wrong."

"You're right about that. The first part, I mean!"

Elena Morgan came in just as he spoke. There was an awkward silence for a few seconds. Kiki had learned early in the year not to talk about anything but *Courier* business when she was in the office. Elena had big ears and a big mouth.

"Feeling better?" Kiki asked, attempting to fill the void.

Elena brushed aside the question with a wave of her hand and sat down at her desk. "Of all the people you could have sent to the Galliard," she said to Andrew, "you had to pick the one person who has no background in the arts at all! Couldn't you have found one of our roving reporters?"

"She's feeling better," Kiki muttered. "You can always count on Elena for affirmation!"

Elena swiveled around in her chair. "Well, you must admit you're more at home in the gym than you are in a museum!"

"Maybe so," said Kiki. "But I don't have to like every assignment I get. How did you know that I went, anyway?"

"Dr. Van Kayser had dinner with us on Saturday night," said Elena smugly. "My mother is on the Board of Trustees, you know."

"No, I didn't know," said Kiki. "I'll file it in my Important Information Bank."

"I can't believe you'd question him about that forgery they found in the collection. How embarrassing! And unprofessional! The man's doing us a favor, and you drag that out."

"Lay off, Elena," Andrew said. "Reporters aren't supposed to ask easy questions."

"Well, if we do a follow-up," Elena said, "I'll do it. Dr. Van Kayser is giving me an internship next week during spring break, so I'll have lots of opportunities to do another interview."

"An internship?" Kiki asked. Her interest in the possibility of an internship overrode the snide remarks. "I didn't know they had internships there!"

"They never have before," said Elena. "I'll be the first intern in the history of the museum. I'll be working directly with Dr. Van Kayser, and Mr. Dartmouth has already promised to give me credit in history class for it."

"Bully for you," Kiki mumbled.

The bell rang and Kiki picked up her backpack. "I could have gone all day without that news," she said to Andrew when they got into the hall. "See you at lunch."

Kiki sat through first-period English, staring out the window. How unfair that Elena should get an internship when that was exactly what Kiki needed to gain access to the museum.

"Those are the breaks," Andrew said to her in the cafeteria at lunchtime. "I don't know what you can do about it."

"Well, I know!" Kiki said. "Mrs. Kendrick's on that board. Maybe she can pull some strings. I'll talk to her tonight—I'm babysitting for Jeffrey."

"It's worth a try," Andrew agreed, "but I wouldn't go around telling any of the trustees why you want to work there. If they hired the guy, they must have confidence in him."

"What do you think I am?" Kiki said. "Stupid?"

"No, not stupid—just jealous!"

Kiki stormed out of the cafeteria, went outside, and sat on the concrete steps leading to the main doors until the bell rang. She didn't get mad at Andrew very often. Maybe he was right. Maybe she *was* jealous of Elena. For a lot of reasons, not just because she was getting an internship at the museum. Elena was pretty—beautiful, actually—with long black

28

hair, deep blue eyes, and a figure that looked like it came right out of a magazine. And she wrote a weekly column, "Morgan's Musings," for *The Courier* with almost no restrictions on subject matter. Kiki really wanted to write a column . . . and she would gladly trade her red hair and freckles for Elena's sophisticated look if she could . . . and she wanted to get an internship at the Galliard!

Well, that was the one thing she might be able to swing.

She saw Andrew briefly after her last class and apologized.

"Forget it," he said. "What are friends for if you can't yell at them?" He took a notepad out of his back pocket and pretended to be checking something. "Let's see, counting today, I'm twenty-two screaming fits behind. If I put them back to back, I could probably yell at you for a whole week. Now that's something I could really get into!"

Kiki punched his arm. "Cut it out, Carlisle."

"Talk to you later," he said, riding off on his bike with a group of boys. "Good luck with Mrs. Kendrick!"

After dinner Kiki and Pumpkin walked to the Kendricks' house. Two-year-old Jeffrey met them at the door in his sleepers and took immediate possession of the cat.

"He's been waiting all day to play with Pumpkin," Mrs. Kendrick called to Kiki. She came out of the bedroom carrying her coat. "There are some chocolate chip cookies in the kitchen. Lorne and I should get home about the same time," she said. "I'll be at the Sloanes' playing bridge—he's at the office working. You have the Sloanes' number, right?"

Kiki nodded. The Sloanes lived just down the street. She looked again at Mrs. Kendrick, who seemed to be in a hurry. Suddenly, Kiki felt shy about asking her about the internship. She wasn't into art or history that much—the only reason she wanted to get a placement at the museum was because of what Gabrielle had told her, and because she didn't like Dr. Van Kayser.

Her mother's words replayed in her mind. *"I go with my gut feeling . . ."*

"Mrs. Kendrick," Kiki said, "do you think I could get an internship at the Galliard Museum?"

Susan Kendrick turned from the entry-hall mirror and smiled at her. "Why, Kiki! I didn't know you were interested in the museum!"

"Well, I interviewed Dr. Van Kayser on Saturday, for an article in the school newspaper. And . . . and I just thought I'd like to learn more," Kiki finished lamely.

"Well, I'll certainly be glad to bring it up with the board," said Mrs. Kendrick. "We meet on Thursday. But I don't think we've ever had interns before."

"A girl from our school will be there next week during spring break."

"Well, if the precedent has been set, I can't see any reason why they wouldn't consider you. We couldn't pay you for your time, but it would be valuable experience. I'd be happy to sponsor you, Kiki! I'll let you know on Thursday what happens." She gave Kiki a quick hug, kissed Jeffrey, patted Pumpkin, and was out the door.

"I can't believe it!" Kiki said to herself. "I can't believe it! It was so easy!" She danced a few steps on the tile floor of the entry hall and made faces at herself in the mirror until she realized that two pairs of eyes were quizzically watching her performance.

She whirled around, crouched down, and faced them, nose to nose. "And it's off to the kitchen for all creatures!" she roared in a fake fierce voice. "Where chocolate chip cookies await the *good* children and animals!" The child and the cat sprinted down the hall giggling and meowing, with Kiki in hot pursuit.

"Jeffrey feed Pumpkin!" Jeffrey said, reaching up for a cookie for the cat. Over the past few months, Kiki had become the first-choice sitter for the son of the county's new district attorney and his wife, and Jeffrey and Pumpkin were fast friends.

Knowing Pumpkin's passion for chocolate, Mrs. Kendrick always made sure that there were cookies or cupcakes available when Kiki and her cat came over. But that night Pumpkin was acting strange. Even though Jeffrey had diligently picked the chocolate chips out of the cookie—which was routine procedure—Pumpkin was not cooperating. He'd take the proferred chocolate chip on the tip of his pink tongue and immediately spit it out on the floor.

"Kitty sick?" Jeffrey asked, looking up at Kiki.

"He must be," she replied. "I've never seen him refuse chocolate chips before. This is a first!"

She got Jeffrey settled in bed by eight o'clock and started her homework. Pumpkin went off to Mr. Kendrick's home office in a back room and made himself comfortable on the papers in the wastebasket—one of his favorite hiding places. Kiki was so excited about the possibility of getting an internship that she had trouble concentrating on her math. At about nine o'clock she gave up trying and dialed Andrew's number. The phone rang and rang. Not only was no one home, the Carlisles had even forgotten to turn on the answering machine.

When Mrs. Kendrick got home around ten, Kiki was curled up on a floor cushion, watching television.

"Did everything go okay?" she asked as she hung up her coat in the hall closet.

"Yup," said Kiki. "No problems, no phone calls."

Alerted by the sound of their voices, Pumpkin wandered sleepily out of the back room, blinking at the bright lights.

"Well, no problem with Jeffrey, that is," Kiki said. "Believe it or not, Pumpkin refused to eat the chocolate chips!"

"You're kidding!" Mrs. Kendrick said.

"Nope. It's a first. I've never seen him refuse chocolate in any form before. He just spit out the chips."

"Wait a minute," Mrs. Kendrick said. "Let me try something." She walked to the kitchen, and Kiki and the cat followed. She took a canister from the shelf, pulled out a bag of chocolate chips, and offered one to Pumpkin.

He sniffed warily, and then picked the chip up on his tongue, rolled it around in his mouth, swallowed, and begged for another.

Kiki laughed. "You really have the magic touch! He wouldn't take one from Jeffrey or from me!"

"Well, I'll let you in on a little secret," said Mrs. Kendrick. "I was feeding him *real* chocolate chips. You were feeding him carob chips from some cookies my sister brought with her over the weekend. She's allergic to chocolate, so she substitutes carob."

"Fake chocolate! I couldn't tell!" Kiki said with a smile. "How could he?"

"Some well-developed animal instinct, I guess." Mrs. Kendrick reached down and stroked Pumpkin's back. "I'll never try to put one over on you again," she said, feeding him another real chocolate chip. "Nothing but the real McCoy for you, Pumpkin! You've got class!"

She walked to the door with Kiki. "I'll call you Thursday afternoon about the internship," she said.

"Thanks!"

Kiki and Pumpkin sprinted the short block to the Colliers' house.

* * *

It seemed like a month till Thursday—not that Kiki didn't have plenty to keep her occupied. For one thing, *The Courier* was published every Friday during the school year, and Thursday was always bedlam in the office. This week Andrew was doing layout and pasteup while Kiki put the final touches on her article about Dr. Van Kayser. Elena, as usual, retreated into "creative mode" while finishing her column. This week's was about the influence of color on a person's mood—inspired, Kiki was sure, by Elena's recent trip to a local department store to have her color chart done.

"Come on, Elena," Andrew pleaded, looking at his watch. "I want to get home before morning."

Elena closed her eyes and shook her head as if he were interrupting some major thought process. She opened them, typed a few lines—cautiously pecking at the keys to avoid chipping her new bright red nail polish—and stared into space.

"Black," Kiki whispered to Andrew, giggling as they watched and waited for Elena's next spurt of inspiration to hit. "The mood of the moment is black."

"Shut up," Andrew whispered back, rolling

his eyes. "You just don't appreciate creative genius. You need an attitude adjustment."

"I need dinner," Kiki said in a normal voice. She gathered up her books. "And a phone call from the Kendricks. Anything else you want done around here?"

"No," said Andrew. "Go ahead. 'Morgan's Musings' is the last piece of copy I need."

"Then I'm outta here," said Kiki. "Wish me luck!"

"If you're thinking you need luck to get an internship at the Galliard, you're right," said Elena, coming sharply back to reality.

Kiki looked from Elena to Andrew, who shook his head.

"Not me," Andrew said. "I didn't say a word." Kiki had told Andrew that she'd asked Mrs. Kendrick to petition the board, but they had agreed not to say anything around Elena.

"Your little copycat scheme to get an internship at the museum didn't work," Elena continued. "My mother is secretary of the board. When Mrs. Kendrick called her last night to get her request on the agenda, my mother told her in no uncertain terms that she would not vote in favor of two intern- ships." Elena flipped her long black hair over her shoulder and gave Kiki a saccharine smile. "She also told her that Dr. Van Kayser would back her up. Maybe you'll have a chance in the summer, or next year, but the first internship is *mine*."

Kiki swallowed hard and picked up her backpack. "Your mother doesn't speak for the whole board," she snapped. She strode to the door, not wanting Elena to see her disappointment. "See you tomorrow, Andrew." She ran down the stairs and out to the bike racks, angry that Elena knew she had talked to Mrs. Kendrick, and discouraged that she had opposition. *So what if there are two interns?* she thought. *What's the difference? It's not like they're paying us.*

She parked her bike in the garage and entered through the side door, heading straight for the answering machine on the kitchen counter. There were three messages. She was rewinding the tape to replay them when there was a thump and some scratching at the side door, announcing Pumpkin as he squeezed through his private entrance—a small opening cut in the lower half of the door. He marched over to Kiki and rubbed up against her leg, meowing piteously.

"Well, well, if it isn't Pumpkin. Don't tell *me* your troubles," she said, contradicting her tone of voice by reaching down and ruffling his fur. "I've got enough of my own. Besides, any cat who disappears for two days without leaving a note doesn't deserve sympathy. You know we're big on notes around here!"

Eeoow! Pumpkin stretched lazily to full length with his front legs flat on the floor, back curved, and rump in the air. As usual, he didn't look any thinner for his days out of the house. *Eeoow!* He pawed at her jeans with one outstretched foot.

Kiki found it hard to maintain her gloomy mood with her pet begging for attention. She stooped over and picked him up and buried her face in his fur. "The phantom cat returns!" she said. "Where have you been this time?"

Now and then, Pumpkin would simply disappear. The first time it had happened, Kiki and her mother had searched the neighborhood until midnight looking for him, and Kiki had been sure that he was gone forever. She had had visions of a petless family in a car picking him up and taking him away, or a cranky animal hater calling the animal control truck to come and get him or, worse yet, him being injured by a car and slinking off into someone's shrubbery to die. Dr. Collier had taken her down to the city pound the next morning, where they looked at dozens of stray cats, but Pumpkin hadn't been there.

Miraculously, he had reappeared forty-eight hours later, showing up for dinner as though he had never left, and looking none the worse for his travels.

In time, as Pumpkin's mysterious departures became regular occurrences, Kiki stopped worrying and became curious about where he went. She and Andrew had made a game out of speculating on Pumpkin's adventures. Was he training undercover cats? Having a tryst with some gorgeous lady cat friend? Solving a mystery that had baffled local authorities? Performing some secret act of bravery, relying on his sixth sense? Visiting another planet? Freeing all the cats at the city pound? Inspecting the state's largest chocolate factory? Or just relaxing on a beach somewhere?

Of course, when she thought back, Pumpkin had originally come to her in a mysterious way, showing up at the bike rack at the junior high one day as if he was simply returning to his owner.

"This time," she said to the cat, pulling him up into her lap, "you were sitting in on the meeting of the museum's Board of Trustees, right? And you voted in favor of two internships." She giggled. "And you bit Mrs. Morgan on the way out, right?"

Pumpkin purred and snuggled up against her as she pushed the button on the answering machine. The first message was from an insurance salesman. The second was from her mom, saying she'd be late getting home. The third was from Mrs. Kendrick.

Kiki listened to the last message a second time. "Hi, Kiki! This is Susan Kendrick. It's four-ten. Give me a call when you get home."

Was her tone of voice positive or negative? Kiki couldn't tell. She punched in the Kendricks' number and waited. One ring. Two. Three. Just as the fourth ring began, Mrs. Kendrick answered.

"Hi," said Kiki. "It's me, Kiki."

"Hi!" said Mrs. Kendrick. "Thanks for calling back." There was a noise in the background, and Kiki could hear Jeffrey crying. "Whoops! Time out," said Mrs. Kendrick. She put down the receiver and Kiki fidgeted, wanting to know and yet not wanting to know what had happened at the board meeting. Pumpkin wiggled free from her grasp and pawed at the phone, exhibiting the same impatience that Kiki was feeling. Finally Mrs. Kendrick came back on the line.

"Sorry," she said, laughing. "Just a minor catastrophe. Well, Kiki, I've got some good news and some bad news. The bad news is that Dr. Van Kayser told the board this afternoon that he wouldn't have time to supervise two student interns next week. So I'm sorry, you won't be able to work out of his office. He said he might be able to take on a student in the summer."

Disappointment welled up inside Kiki, almost blotting out Mrs. Kendrick's explanation about the curator's time crunch, which was caused by a fundraiser and the anticipated arrival of a touring collection, both scheduled for that month.

"Well, thanks for trying," Kiki murmured. *Good thing there's only one day of school left before spring break*, she thought. *I wouldn't be able to put up with Elena's smugness for more than a day.*

"But that's just the bad news!" said Mrs. Kendrick brightly. "The good news is that one of the members of the board—Dr. Allenby, who works with your mother at the hospital—suggested that you might be willing to take an internship with Mrs. Janssen in the restoration lab. That way, Dr. Van Kayser would only be responsible for one student. Would that be okay with you?"

Kiki could hardly believe what she was hearing!

"Dr. Allenby says he knows you," Mrs. Kendrick went on.

"Yes, he's a pediatrician," Kiki said. "He's been my doctor since I was born."

"Well, the board agreed that one student in administration and one in the restoration studio would be fine with them. How do you feel about working with Mrs. Janssen?" She paused. "She's from the old school. You'll learn a lot, but she may be pretty strict. I hear she's not all that easy to get along with."

"Oh, that's okay. That's great!" Kiki said. "In fact, it's perfect! I met her on Saturday. I'd rather be in her studio than in administration, anyway."

"Oh, I'm so glad!" said Mrs. Kendrick. "Well, you can show up for work Monday morning at nine. Report to Mrs. Janssen."

Kiki thanked her twice and hung up, then grabbed Pumpkin and danced him around the kitchen. "Perfect! Perfect! Perfect!" she chanted to the astonished cat, who seized the first opportunity to escape from her grasp and retreated to the top of the microwave on the counter.

Kiki rushed back over to the phone and dialed Andrew's number. "You won't believe it!" she said when he picked up the phone. "I got an internship, too! Ms. Color-Coded Morgan and I will both be toiling in the halls of the Galliard next week!"

But what Kiki couldn't foresee was that her internship was going to be quite different from Elena's—more interesting, and much more dangerous.

Chapter Four

On Monday morning Kiki rode the city bus to the museum. As she was getting off across the street from the Galliard, she saw Elena, dressed in a pink suit and heels—very mature-looking, Kiki thought, and probably borrowed from her mother—getting out of her mother's car in front of the building.

Kiki looked down at her blue jeans and tennis shoes, made a face, and decided she'd made the right choice for the restoration studio. She crossed the street and entered the building.

"The museum opens at ten," the woman at the reception desk said.

"I'm an intern," Kiki replied, giving the woman her name. "I'm to report to Mrs. Janssen in the restoration lab."

The woman consulted some papers on a clipboard and nodded. "Oh, yes. Go to the end of the hall and take the stairway down. The studio is on your left."

Kiki hurried down the stairs and rapped at the studio door.

"Come in!"

Gabrielle Janssen was hunched over the workbench, with a bright light focused on the object in her hand. "The tweezers," she said, groping on the bench for something. She didn't turn her head. Kiki hurried over and handed her the instrument that she seemed to be looking for. Gabrielle still did not look up. She was holding a pendant in her hand that appeared to be made of fine gold threads. Her thick glasses were pushed up on her forehead and she had a jeweler's eyepiece protruding from one eye.

"There!" she said, setting the pendant down with a pleased expression. She took the loupe from her eye and slipped her glasses down into place. "Ah, Kiki," she said. "Why did you not tell me last week when you were here that you would be working with me?"

"I didn't know until Thursday afternoon, Gabrielle," Kiki said. "I—"

"It does not matter," said Gabrielle, brushing aside her explanation. "Dr. Van Kayser came to me this morning with the news. You are here and you will learn. But we will have some rules, yes? First, while we are in the studio, I am the teacher and you are the student. Yes?"

"Yes, of course."

"And while we are working, I am Mrs. Janssen, yes?"

"Yes, okay," said Kiki, confused by Gabrielle's sudden formality. "Except you said last week that I should call you Gabrielle."

"Yes, but last week you were not my student."

"Right, but . . ." *Is this what Mrs. Kendrick meant when she said she'd heard that Gabrielle is not easy to get along with?* Kiki wondered.

"Good. We understand each other. I am Mrs. Janssen, you are Collier. And where is your Pumpkin?" She pronounced his name *Pump-keen*, stressing the first syllable.

"He's at home. I didn't think I should bring him."

"You may bring him. It is good that a student should have a companion to listen to complaints. And he is acquainted with Monet."

At the mention of his name, the heavyset dog materialized from the shadows in the corner and lumbered over to Gabrielle's side, where he let out a deep sigh and sank to the floor.

Kiki smiled. "I don't plan to have any complaints."

"But you will," said Gabrielle seriously. She smiled at Kiki. "Are you ready to go to work now?"

Kiki nodded. "Yes," she said softly. She was puzzled by this unexpected change in Gabrielle, and finally decided it was because Dr. Van Kayser hadn't given her any advance notice. But he had known since Thursday that Kiki would be interning in the restoration studio. Why hadn't he told Gabrielle sooner? Had it been an oversight, or had it been deliberate? Kiki's mind flashed back to the conversation she'd had with the older woman the last time she had been there. Did Gabrielle think she was here to spy on her? Did she think Kiki really was a friend of Dr. Van Kayser?

Gabrielle pulled a stool out from under the far end of the workbench and switched on a hanging overhead light. "You will sit here," she said. She walked to a shelf on the back wall of the studio and picked up an armful of dusty periodicals. "You will read, Collier," she said, putting the stack of magazines on the counter.

Kiki looked first at the stack and then at Gabrielle. "What do you want me to read?" she asked.

"Everything," said Gabrielle. Her voice was pleasant but firm.

Kiki opened the periodical on the top of the pile. The issue was devoted to a scholarly comparison of sculpture through the ages, the different materials used (stone, metal, clay, glass, synthetics) and the two major classifications: carved, or cut-down sculpture, and modeled, or built-up sculpture. While Kiki read, Gabrielle was quietly busy at the other end of the workbench. Occasionally Kiki would look up from the magazine to see what the woman was doing. A small oil painting was propped up on an easel in front of her, and Gabrielle was patiently mixing blue paint in tiny dabs on a sheet of glass about twelve inches square. At one point Gabrielle caught her glance and smiled at her. Finally she spoke.

"Come here, Collier," she said. Kiki slid off the stool, grateful for the opportunity to stop reading.

Using a long, fragile-looking paintbrush as a pointer, Gabrielle indicated a small scratch on the painting. "This we must repair," she said. She held the glass palette up to the light.

"Which one would you choose?" she asked Kiki.

Kiki looked for a long time as the strong light shone on the dabs of blue paint. At first she thought they all looked the same, but the more she studied them the more her eye could distinguish a slight variance. She looked at the blue around the scratch on the painting and back at the palette. "I think that one," she said, pointing.

"You have a good eye," said Gabrielle, nodding her approval. "It is almost the right choice. I will use this one." She pointed to the dab next to the one Kiki had chosen. "It has a trace more of the red." She delicately applied the paint to the scratch and, with a few deft strokes, blended the color.

"It's perfect, Gabr—Mrs. Janssen!" Kiki said. "I can't even tell where the scratch was!"

Gabrielle smiled at her. "It is time for us to have a coffee break," she said, putting the brush in a shallow container of turpentine. "I will treat you. The coffee shop is on the main floor."

Gabrielle locked the door to the studio and led the way up the stairs, across the rotunda, and through one of the exhibit rooms to the coffee shop, which was really an indoor-outdoor cafeteria with a main dining area and a narrow veranda set with wrought-iron tables and chairs.

"The weather is still cool, but pleasant," said Gabrielle. "We will go out to the veranda."

She ordered coffee for herself and a soda for Kiki and carried the tray outside. As they passed through the almost-empty dining room, Kiki noticed Elena and Dr. Van Kayser sitting at a table by the wall. Neither one acknowledged their presence, although Kiki was sure Elena had looked up as they came in.

"This afternoon," Gabrielle said after they had chatted for a while, "we will visit the charm and mystery of the Egyptian collection. What do you know about Egyptian relics, Kiki?" Kiki was startled at first to hear Gabrielle use her given name and was relieved that the teacher-student relationship wasn't quite so formal out of the studio.

"Not much," Kiki said. "Our history class watched a video about King Tut when the exhibition was touring the United States, but that's all."

"That is a good beginning," said Gabrielle. "We have nothing that grand here, of course, but we have a respectable exhibit. And as a cat lover, you will have much in common with the Egyptians!" She pushed her chair away from the table and stood up. "Time to get back to our work," she said.

The rest of the morning passed slowly for Kiki as she continued her reading and Gabrielle cleaned a small bronze statue. Looking forward to the afternoon's visit to the museum's Egyptian collection, Kiki thumbed through the periodicals searching for an article about Egypt's history, but had no success.

At noon, Gabrielle brought a large brown paper bag from under the workbench and announced it was time for lunch.

"Did you bring lunch with you?" she asked.

"Yes," Kiki replied. "I brought a sandwich and an apple."

"Good," said Gabrielle. "We can go back up to the cafeteria and get something to drink and sit out on the veranda to eat. They won't be busy today. The museum is usually closed on Mondays, except during the weeks that school is out."

Kiki noticed when they got to the cafeteria that Elena and Dr. Van Kayser were having lunch at the same table they had occupied earlier.

"You know her?" Gabrielle asked, nodding her head toward Elena.

"Yes," Kiki replied. "She's from my school."

"But you don't like her," said Gabrielle. She said this as a statement more than a question.

"Not particularly," said Kiki. "She's doing an internship this week, too. With Dr. Van Kayser. Her mother's on the Board of Trustees. She was the one who was really supposed to come interview Dr. Van Kayser for the paper last week."

"Her mother is the woman with that rouge and the black eyebrows with purple lids?" Gabrielle asked, taking the food from her bag.

Kiki grinned. That was a pretty accurate description of Mrs. Morgan. "That's the one," she said.

"Here," said Gabrielle. "We will share." She pushed a chicken leg toward Kiki. "I have two. And lots of vegetables." She put a plastic bag full of celery and carrot sticks, broccoli flowerets, and cherry tomatoes at Kiki. "Not as good as my own," she said. "Come summer I will have good vegetables."

"Do you have a garden?" Kiki asked, offering Gabrielle half of her cheese sandwich.

"Thank you," Gabrielle said. "A garden? I have a farm!" she continued, laughing. "Most of my acreage is rented to a farmer, but I keep enough land to grow my vegetables. I like working in the dirt, seeing things grow. You must come to my place and visit, Kiki! I will take you in my van some night after work."

"I'd like that," said Kiki.

On the way back to the restoration studio, Gabrielle detoured up to one of the third-floor exhibit rooms. "I must look at something," she explained to Kiki. She walked to a wall of shelves protected by a locked glass panel, inserted a key, and slid the panel aside. The shelves were filled with white porcelain pieces with Chinese markings and jade figurines. A brass plate said *Yuan Dynasty, 1279–1368 A.D.* Gabrielle picked up a gracefully rounded bowl and gently examined it. She turned it to the light, her fingers touching each part: the curve of the bowl, the rim, the base.

While Gabrielle was examining the bowl Kiki wandered over to a glass case that held a sixth-century bronze Buddha and an ugly bronze hippopotamus with jeweled eyes which, according to the card beside it, were emeralds.

"Collier!"

Gabrielle's voice was sharp, and Kiki hurried over to her. "Hold this!" the woman said, thrusting the bowl at her.

Nervously, Kiki took the precious museum

piece in both hands and looked at Gabrielle for further instruction.

"Have you become acquainted with it?"

"Uh . . ."

Gabrielle reached out for the bowl and replaced it on the shelf. Picking up a slim, elegant porcelain vase that sat beside it, she handed it to Kiki, who realized that she was being tested but was unsure of what she was learning.

"There is a difference! What is the difference?"

Kiki looked at the squat bowl on the shelf and back at the vase in her hands.

"No, no! Do not look at the objects! Feel them!"

Kiki dropped her eyes and felt the vase.

"The difference?" Gabrielle repeated impatiently.

Kiki shrugged. "Well, this one feels cold," she volunteered hesitantly.

Gabrielle beamed. "That is right!" she said. She put the vase back in the case and locked it. "Come," she said. "You will read some more, and at four we will visit the Valley of the Nile."

Kiki was beginning to regret her haste in asking for an internship. If Dr. Van Kayser was a fraud, she certainly wasn't going to have a chance to expose him if she spent all her time in the restoration lab reading dusty scholarly journals.

Gabrielle unlocked the door to the lab and turned on the light. Kiki went to her stool at the end of the workbench and picked up the magazine on sculpture, comforted only by the knowledge that later in the afternoon they would tour the Egyptian exhibit.

"No, no, Collier," Gabrielle said, taking the magazine from her hands. "I have something exciting for you to read." She took a book from a shelf under the bench, flipped through several pages, and handed it to Kiki. "You start reading there." She put a finger on the page. Kiki looked at the chapter heading: *Porcelain: Formulae and Firing Temperatures*. Not exactly her idea of exciting reading! She looked up at Gabrielle for some hint of what she was supposed to find, but the restorer was already absorbed in mixing some vile-smelling concoction in a metal bucket.

Kiki read for twenty minutes. She became acquainted with hard paste, kaolin clay, underglaze, firing temperatures for different types of porcelain, and European attempts to duplicate Chinese porcelain. She was almost at the end of the chapter when she let out a shout.

"Gabrielle! Mrs. Janssen! That bowl in the Chinese collection. It's a fake!"

Gabrielle turned and smiled at her. "Why?" she asked.

"It's probably soft paste," Kiki said, surprising even herself.

"Why?"

"Because compared to the vase, it felt warm. So the vase is hard paste—kaolin clay. It's genuine Chinese porcelain, but the bowl is probably European."

"That is right, Collier. Very good. There are other tests that could be applied. For instance, the glaze on the bowl would scratch if it was an imitation, and if we broke it, the underglaze colors in the pattern would be found also in the bisque."

Kiki looked at Gabrielle, puzzled. "Wait a minute," she said. "You knew ahead of time that the bowl was a fake. What's it doing in the Chinese collection if it's a forgery?"

"I would also like to know the answer to that, Kiki," Gabrielle said, dropping her teacher's role. "I have requested the information from the curator, but he has not responded. Perhaps if I send you upstairs with a note, repeating the request, he will give me the information I need."

"Why would he give it to me?" Kiki said.

"How did you get your internship?" Gabrielle countered, smiling.

"Well, because Mrs. Kendrick and Dr. Allenby . . . oh, I get it!" Kiki could feel her excitement mounting. "He can threaten to fire you, but he can't fire me because I'm not an employee. And if he refuses to give you information while I'm here, I might tell my two friends on the Board of Trustees!" Kiki laughed. "That's like blackmail!"

"It is similar," said Gabrielle, smiling as she reached for a notepad and pencil. "But it is not for personal gain."

Chapter Five

Kiki's excitement mounted as she rode the elevator to the curator's third-floor office. Would he refuse to give her the information that Gabrielle had asked for?

She walked down the hall, rapped on the door, and waited. A few moments later the door opened. Elena gave her a haughty look. "Yes, Kiki?" she said.

"Mrs. Janssen needs some information about a bowl in the Chinese collection," Kiki said. "Is Dr. Van Kayser here?"

"No, but I can handle that," Elena said smugly. "He explained the catalog system to me." Kiki handed her the note and Elena stepped back inside the office.

Kiki followed and watched as Elena went into an anteroom that was lined with small drawers, much like a library catalog. Soon she came out with a card in her hand.

"You'll have to copy the information. I can't

allow any of the cards to leave the office," she said, flaunting her position of authority. "Especially down to the basement. Dr. Van Kayser told me all about that woman down there. I'm sure you're getting a terrific education!" she added sarcastically.

"What do you mean by that crack?" Kiki asked.

Elena smiled. "She won't be on the payroll much longer. Dr. Van Kayser is going to ask the board to release her next month. I mean, the last thing a museum needs is a forger-in-residence. He told me all about her 'finding' that forgery while he was in London. She actually switched the pieces!"

Kiki's face flushed. "How dare you say that about Gabrielle!" She picked up a pen from the ornate coffee table and started to copy information from the card to the back of Gabrielle's note. But her hand stiffened as she read the words on the card.

Elena drummed her fingers impatiently as she waited. "Well, are you going to write it or aren't you?" she snapped.

"I don't have to write it," Kiki said, flipping the card back on the table and hurrying to the door. "It will be easy to remember."

"Dr. Van Kayser knows what that woman's up to," Elena yelled after her. "She's just trying to discredit him because she wants his job!"

Kiki stormed out of the office and down the hall to the elevator. She fumed all the way down to the main floor and wheeled out of the elevator so abruptly that she almost crashed into two women waiting to go up.

"Sorry," Kiki muttered.

When she got back down to the restoration lab, Gabrielle was packing some things in a crate.

She looked up at Kiki. "Well?" she asked.

"The bowl came from a private collection in Boston," Kiki said through clenched teeth. "And it was authenticated by Stottmeier and Dresler of Amsterdam."

Gabrielle raised a bushy eyebrow. "I suspected so," she said. "He has found another way to line his pockets."

"Stottmeier," Kiki said. "That was Van Kayser's name when you first knew him."

"Yes. The company is owned by his cousin. They are—how do you say it?—in cahoots. Ludwig commissions a clever forgery and buys it for a fraction of the cost of the authentic piece. His cousin appraises the forged item at full value, it is put into this private collection, which is actually Van Kayser's, and after an appropriate length of time, Van

Kayser sells it for a very large sum of money to unsuspecting collectors and museums. And he has another scheme for dealing with items that are already in the museum: he has copies made and substitutes them."

"That's fraud! That's grand larceny!" Kiki said. "Can't you just call the police?"

"Not yet," said Gabrielle, turning back to her packing. "I must have more proof. You read, Collier! There is much to learn!"

That's the understatement of the year, Kiki thought as she unwillingly went back to the pile of reading material. There was no way she could concentrate on the academic articles when there was so much intrigue right here at the museum. *The curator is a thief!* She'd have a lot to tell Andrew that night when she got home. She was glad that she could bring Pumpkin with her the next day. For all his weird ways, the orange cat was a good friend to have around when strange things were going on.

Kiki debated telling Gabrielle what Elena had told her, and decided against it. No point in making things worse. She'd hear the rumor soon enough.

"You are reading upside down, Collier!" Gabrielle said with a hint of humor in her voice. Startled, Kiki quickly righted the magazine in her hand. "It is time, I think, to go and visit Egypt."

Kiki's concerns slipped away as Gabrielle guided her through the treasures of Egypt, providing such rich descriptions of individual pieces in the collection that Kiki could imagine herself living in the culture of that faraway place and time.

Elegant white alabaster ointment jars, carved to represent animal- and humanlike deities, jeweled gold necklaces, and beaded earrings that would reach to the shoulder of the wearer caught Kiki's attention, especially when Gabrielle explained that the *udjat* eye, engraved on several pieces of jewelry, was believed to be a powerful amulet against sickness, and was actually thought to be capable of restoring the dead to life.

"Do you believe that?" Kiki asked.

Gabrielle turned to face her. "There are many things in life that we do not understand," she said seriously. "To deny belief is to limit possibility. To limit possibility is to live in a small world, with yourself at the center. That is not good." She jammed her hand into her pocket and pulled out a ring strung on a piece of black cord.

She nodded toward the display. "When Roland bought these for the collection, he personally paid for this ring. It is not museum quality because it is damaged. But I carry it always."

Kiki took the ring from her hand and turned it over. The *udjat* eye etched in the center stared up at her, unblinking.

"Couldn't it have saved *his* life?" Kiki asked.

"Perhaps it did," said Gabrielle. "Perhaps he lived longer because we had it. Perhaps he lives now elsewhere in the universe. We do not know. It is a possibility." She put the ring back in her pocket and moved on to another part of the exhibit—the sarcophagus, the ornate coffin that held the mummy of a woman of royal descent who had lived over three thousand years ago. Standing guard at the foot of the sarcophagus was a regal-looking cat, carved in ebony and posed in stately splendor on an alabaster pedestal.

"His face looks like Pumpkin's," Kiki said, "but the rest of him isn't fat enough!"

"Cats were worshiped in ancient Egypt," Gabrielle explained. "They even had a cat-headed goddess named Bast."

"Don't tell Pumpkin," Kiki said with a grin. "He'll start thinking he's not being treated well enough!"

"Archaeologists have found cat mummies," Gabrielle continued, "with mouse mummies inside the sarcophagus to provide food for the cats in another life."

A buzzer sounded, and Gabrielle looked quickly at her watch. "It is closing time," she said. "We have fifteen minutes to leave the building before the alarm system is activated. I will see you tomorrow. I must get a few things from the studio before I go. Good night!"

Kiki walked to the bus stop, her mind in a whirl over all that had come up in one short eight-hour span. Dr. Collier was home when she arrived, and the nutmeg-cinnamon smell that announced homemade apple pie made Kiki realize she was hungry.

"Hi, hon," her mother called from the kitchen. "How did it go? Fun?"

Kiki smiled a private smile before she came down the hall to the kitchen. If there was one thing she had learned, it was to be selective in telling her mother about the events of the day. She could tell her mom almost anything, but she hated to see her worry.

"Parts of it were fun," she said. She perched on a kitchen stool and watched as a pan of golden-brown chicken exited the oven. "Parts of it were boring. Hey, that looks yummy. You must have gotten home early."

"Went in early, got off early," said Dr. Collier, turning around just in time to see Kiki break a piece of crust off the pie that was cooling on the counter.

"Hands off!" she said, swatting at Kiki with a potholder. "You're not five anymore. You can't start with dessert and get away with it!"

Kiki grinned, and a rush of memories flooded over her. This was the way her mother used to be when her father had been alive—before the accident. Playful, smiling. Her parents had planned their lives around her, taking different shifts at the hospital so one of them could always be with her. It was hard to believe that two years had passed since her father was killed. When that had happened the whole routine changed. Her mother now worked full-time, and Kiki usually ended up being the cook. She liked experimenting in the kitchen, but it was a real treat to come home and find dinner ready to eat.

"I found out something about me today," Kiki said, picking up Pumpkin, who had bounded in from his sentry post on the living room window-sill. "I'd make a good Egyptian. I'm an ailurophile."

"You're a *what*?"

"An ailurophile. A cat lover."

"Sounds like an infectious disease," muttered Dr. Collier. "Soup's on!"

After dinner, while her mother was in the living room reading, Kiki called Andrew and told him about Gabrielle and the forged piece of porcelain and about Elena's accusations.

"It was more exciting than my day," he griped. "My mother made me clean the garage. Just a training exercise, she says! Tomorrow I get to clean my room."

"That'll take the rest of the week," said Kiki, laughing.

"How can you say such a thing?" Andrew asked, feigning indignation. Then he quickly added, "Don't answer that!"

"Well, if you ever get done," said Kiki, "come down to the museum for the afternoon. Gabrielle said it would be okay if you came along on our exhibit tour of the day."

"Good idea. Mom might lighten up if she thought I was getting some culture." He dropped his voice. "I've gotta go. My brother wants the phone. Kiki, watch yourself down there. I mean . . ." He sounded flustered. "You're not even sure who the bad guys are. If you poke around too much, you could be in danger."

Kiki felt her cheeks getting hot. She was glad he couldn't see her blush. "Yeah, I will," she said. "Tomorrow I'm taking Pumpkin. He'll look out for me."

"Sure he will," said Andrew. "Bye."

Kiki replaced the receiver and smiled. It felt funny, but in a good way, to have Andrew concerned about her.

She went to bed early and dreamed she was an Egyptian princess feeding chocolate mice to a sleek ebony cat.

In the morning, Kiki woke to find Pumpkin pulling the blankets and sheets off the bed, as if he knew that he was going with her and was impatient to get on with the adventure.

Chapter Six

When Kiki arrived at the museum, the studio door was unlocked but Gabrielle was not in the room. Pumpkin stalked the room like a hunter, sniffing in the corners, with special attention to Monet's blanket. He let out a resounding sneeze when he investigated the bucket of pungent goop that Gabrielle had mixed the day before.

"That'll teach you to snoop!" Kiki said, laughing. She headed for her stool and switched on the light over the pile of reading material. "Might as well get started," she groused to Pumpkin as she opened a magazine. "Don't miss the next exciting chapter! There, I'm complaining to you already. Gabrielle said I needed a companion to complain to."

Pumpkin jumped to the top of the workbench, looked at her seriously, nose to nose, and then turned and walked the length of the long table, stopping to inspect each item on its surface.

"Get down, Pumpkin," Kiki said, nervously eyeing the objects on the bench. The small painting on the easel was still there, and a copper basket, and some porcelain and glassware at the far end. Pumpkin ignored her, poking at each item, sniffing and pawing, and she stood up to retrieve him. As she did, the orange cat ran to the far end of the bench, arched his back, hissed, and raised his right paw.

"No, Pumpkin!" Kiki yelled, lunging for him. But she wasn't fast enough. The cat hissed again and swung his paw, deliberately pushing something tall and white over the edge. It hit the floor with a *whack*. The cat jumped down and sat on his haunches, proudly surveying the destruction.

"Oh, no," said Kiki under her breath. She dropped to her knees beside the broken object. She recognized it instantly. It was the Yuan-dynasty vase that Gabrielle had taken from the locked case the day before! What was it doing down here, anyway? It was the genuine piece and in mint condition—or at least it had been, until a moment ago. It hadn't needed restoration. Why had Gabrielle brought it down to the studio?

Her heart was thumping and tears blurred her eyes. She should never have brought Pumpkin here. Her mother had questioned it; she had questioned it herself. If it hadn't been Gabrielle's suggestion, she would never have thought of it. And now he had broken a priceless vase. There was no way she could replace it! Kiki started picking up the pieces of porcelain that had shot under the bench on impact. There were surprisingly few. It was as if the fall had crushed the vase, rather than broken it. She cupped it in her hands. In fact, the shattered pieces seemed to be sticking together. The neck hung off to one side, like a dead chicken's in the butcher shop.

Puzzled, Kiki carried the broken vase to the light. Why wasn't it falling apart? She examined it closely. Shards of white porcelain stuck to a white netlike fabric. This wasn't a fourteenth-century Yuan-dynasty vase. This was a twentieth-century reproduction using modern medical supplies! The entire body was reinforced with Marlex!

Her hands cold and trembling, Kiki poked at the broken vase. Elena's accusation that Gabrielle was a forger rang in her ears. *Gabrielle must have made this duplicate*, she thought. *But why?*

There was a sharp knock at the door, and

Kiki whirled around. Pumpkin jumped to the workbench and sat erect, hissing.

"Who is it?" Kiki asked, moving toward the opening door.

"Ah, Miss Collier. I learned at the board meeting that you were to intern with us this week." The curator stood in the doorway, a cold expression on his face.

"Mrs. Janssen isn't here right now," Kiki said quickly, blocking Dr. Van Kayser's entrance. Behind her she could hear a low, ominous rumble coming from Pumpkin's throat.

The man pushed her aside and entered the studio.

"Are you looking for something?" she asked as he walked to the shelves that held artifacts awaiting restoration. *Please don't go near the workbench*, she thought as she followed him. She wished she'd thrown a magazine over the broken vase. *And please, Pumpkin*, she said silently, *don't attack him*.

"I am just looking," he replied, rapidly scanning the shelves. He peered over at the workbench. "My assistant, Miss Morgan, tells me that you were inquiring about a certain Yuan-dynasty object yesterday."

He's looking for the vase, Kiki thought, without replying.

And then he said abruptly, "You needn't tell Mrs. Janssen that I was here."

Pumpkin hissed as the door closed behind him, and Kiki whirled around and let out a deep breath.

"Good Pumpkin! What restraint!" she said. "You didn't attack him!" And then she started to laugh. "Oh, Pumpkin, you're amazing!" The big orange cat was sitting on top of the broken vase like a bird on a nest. His bushy tail was wrapped around his feet so that not one particle of the forged Chinese artifact was visible.

Pumpkin jumped down from the bench and rubbed up against Kiki's leg, and she rewarded him with a slightly melted piece of chocolate from her pocket.

"I see you had an accident here."

Kiki jumped. Gabrielle was standing behind her, holding a large, unframed oil painting. "I have been unloading my van," the restorer continued. "I did not expect you so early."

"I took an early bus," Kiki said. "I—I—Pumpkin knocked this off the bench."

Gabrielle put down the painting and picked up a wastebasket. "It is no loss," she said curtly, sweeping the ruined vase into the wastebasket with her hand. "It was an experiment on my part. Pumpkin was curious, yes?"

"Yes," Kiki said, stammering in her confusion. "I'm sorry, I thought it—"

"It is no loss," Gabrielle repeated.

"Gabrielle . . . um, Mrs. Janssen, Dr. Van Kayser was here a few minutes ago."

The color drained from Gabrielle's face. "But he was scheduled to be in a meeting this morning. Did he see the broken vase?" she asked.

"No," said Kiki. "Pumpkin sat on it."

Her relief was visible. "He is an insightful animal. Let us get to work now, Collier. Today, you will read about Rococo and Baroque paintings." She shuffled through the periodicals as though nothing had happened, and selected a yellowed issue without a cover. "Start here." She turned to a page and put the book down in front of Kiki. Then she busied herself at the workbench. Kiki glanced behind her. Monet and Pumpkin were curled up together on the blanket in the corner.

Kiki tried to read, but had trouble concentrating. Was nothing more going to be said about this? Was Gabrielle also the artisan responsible for the other forgery—the Chinese bowl in the glass case upstairs? But if she was, why would she point it out to Kiki? Was it pride in her work—her *illegal* work?

A thousand questions whirled in Kiki's head for the next hour and a half. When Gabrielle announced it was time for a coffee break, Kiki welcomed the interruption, but not the awkward conversation they exchanged in the cafeteria.

At lunchtime, Kiki told Gabrielle she wasn't hungry and took Pumpkin out to the museum grounds instead of going to the cafeteria. It wasn't a lie—she wasn't hungry. Her stomach was upset and her mind was filled with doubt.

"Forger-in-residence."

It appeared as if Elena was right. What other explanation could there be for the replica of the Yuan-dynasty vase? And Gabrielle certainly had the knowledge and skill to reproduce works of art. Kiki sat down on a concrete bench under a tree on the back lawn of the museum and absent-mindedly stroked Pumpkin. The cat relished the attention and purred appreciatively.

A delivery truck backed into the loading area behind the museum, and Kiki watched as the driver unloaded boxes of potato chips and candy bars and cases of soda for the cafeteria. Maybe she *was* hungry, after all. She took the sandwich from her backpack and nibbled at it, listlessly giving Pumpkin one bite for each one she took. When the sandwich was gone, he wandered off to investigate a hedge that enclosed the property, and Kiki stared at the cars in the small parking lot at the side. An old white van with green curtains at the windows was parked beside a sleek black Cadillac. The van would be Gabrielle's, she decided, and the Cadillac Van Kayser's. She looked at her watch. Almost one o'clock. Time to go back to the studio. Gabrielle had noticed the change in her mood, she was sure, but there was no way she could pretend everything was all right when everything was all wrong.

Kiki stood up and whistled for Pumpkin. It had taken a lot of practice to get him to respond to a whistled summons, but he was finally catching on. Kiki called it another one of his dog tricks—like hiding shoes and burying things in flower beds. She whistled again, and was rewarded with an orange flash racing out from under the hedge. He ran straight toward her until he caught sight of the delivery man steering another load of goods through the back door.

So much for the whistle! "Pumpkin!" Kiki yelled.

The cat glanced at her, wheeled right, and

almost tripped the driver. Then he vaulted up on the loading dock and raced in through the open back door. Kiki started to run. She jumped up on the concrete platform and followed Pumpkin through the opening.

Inside the back of the museum, two halls formed a T. "Your cat went that way, miss!" said the delivery man, laughing. He pointed straight ahead, and Kiki ran in the direction he indicated. A curved archway led directly into one of the smaller exhibit rooms. Kiki stopped and then stepped cautiously into the room, looking around to see if there were any visitors in the area. A sign over the door said *For Emergency Use Only*.

Well, she thought grimly, *this is an emergency.* There was no one in sight. She whistled softly and waited. The room housed the American Indian collection. Ceremonial costumes and headdresses lined the walls; a drum was mounted in a corner; and three glass cases in the center displayed weapons, cooking utensils, pottery, and baskets. On a pedestal beside one of the glass cases was a stunning piece of earthenware with a black and white geometric design. And sitting tall in front of the pedestal, eyes flashing and tail sweeping, was Pumpkin. She reached for the cat and he hissed a warning, reaching out with his right paw to swipe at the pedestal that held the artifact, exactly the way he'd swiped at the Chinese vase in the studio.

"Pumpkin!" she whispered, grabbing him. "You've done enough damage today! You're just lucky the last thing you whacked at was a fake. This one isn't!" She stuffed the protesting cat into her backpack just as a group of visitors, led by a guide, came into the room.

The guide frowned at her. "You must check your backpack at the desk, miss," she said pointedly. "There's no charge." She stopped the group in front of the pedestal. "And this," she explained, "is a rare Pueblo jar."

Kiki gathered up the wiggling backpack in her arms and left the room quickly. She walked through the main rotunda and ran down the stairs to the restoration lab. Gabrielle was already back and busy at the workbench.

"Collier!" she said.

"Yes?" Kiki replied. She caught her breath and set the backpack down on the floor. Pumpkin indignantly huffed his way out and marched over to the blanket, where Monet was taking his afternoon nap.

"This afternoon I will show you how to clean an oil painting," Gabrielle continued. She walked to a rack at the end of the room and extracted a large canvas that portrayed a group of chubby, naked babies playing around a lion that was lying as placidly as a kitten in a green meadow.

"I might have known it would have something to do with a cat," Kiki mumbled.

Gabrielle looked up and smiled. "Pumpkin is giving you problems?" she asked.

Kiki nodded. She felt better seeing Gabrielle smile. "He ran in through the delivery entrance and got into the American Indian exhibit room," Kiki said. "A guide came in with a group of visitors just as I got him stuffed into the backpack. And not a minute too soon! He was about to attack an earthenware pot."

Gabrielle threw her head back and laughed out loud. "Our guides would not know how to deal with such a situation," she said. "Get me the big easel from the corner there. And the bottle of distilled water. You are tired of reading, yes?"

"Sort of," Kiki admitted, smiling. She wished she knew what was going on, but somehow she felt more relaxed than she had since that morning.

"This is an eighteenth-century work," Gabrielle said. "Well done, and not too dirty.

The really filthy paintings come from churches and monasteries where candles are always burning. They have sooty grease on the canvas from burning tallow. Yiich!"

Kiki grinned at Gabrielle's expression of distaste and watched, fascinated, as the woman gently wiped the painting with a sponge dipped in the distilled water. That done, she took a wide paintbrush and applied the gel she had mixed in the bucket.

"We leave this on for three minutes," she instructed, setting a small timer on the workbench, "and then sponge it off with water. If left on too long, it will damage the paint. You may help."

When the timer went off, Kiki took the sponge and carefully started wiping away the cleaning agent. "Look at the difference in the colors!" she said, standing back to admire her work. "I can't believe it's the same painting! The babies are pink now . . . they were yellow before!"

Gabrielle nodded, enjoying her excitement. "There is satisfaction in restoring beauty," she said. "When we are through here, we will go upstairs and visit the art gallery. But first, Collier, get me that paper bag over there. And a section of newspaper. I will—how do you say it?—dispose of the evidence of Pumpkin's accident!"

She upended the wastebasket on the newspaper and wrapped up the broken vase, putting the package in the paper bag. She set the bag in the corner by Money's blanket.

"If someone should visit the studio while we are upstairs, I would not want this to be seen."

Kiki frowned. "Who would visit the studio?" she asked.

Gabrielle shrugged. "Dr. Van Kayser is the only other person with a key," she replied. "But Monet does not like him, so I think he will not come."

Kiki found it hard to picture Monet as a protector. And she wished Gabrielle had not reminded her of the incident with the vase. "Mrs. Janssen, my friend Andrew might come this afternoon. Is that still okay? You said yesterday—"

"But certainly! And I was thinking at lunchtime, would you like to come to my farm today after work? Your friend, he could come, too!"

"I'd have to call my mother," Kiki said.

"Of course. And you tell her I will bring you home at a good time. Not too late. We will stop and get a pizza. We will have a party!"

"Okay," said Kiki. "I'll ask Andrew."

When she and Gabrielle came up from the basement, they found Andrew waiting in the rotunda. Kiki introduced Gabrielle, who promptly took Andrew's hand and shook it enthusiastically. Their tour of the gallery lasted almost until five o'clock. When the buzzer sounded, Kiki and Andrew went to the pay phone just outside the cafeteria, and Gabrielle went downstairs to the studio to get Pumpkin and Monet.

"I will meet you in the parking lot," she said as they headed for the phone.

"She's cool," said Andrew.

"Sort of," said Kiki. "I really like her . . . but I don't know what to think. Andrew, she really could be the forger!" She blurted out the story of the broken Chinese vase. "And then before we left, she hid the pieces so nobody would find them."

Andrew shrugged. "I'd probably do the same thing," he said. "Don't jump to conclusions. It might be perfectly legit. Maybe we'll find out more when we get to her place."

Permission obtained, the two teenagers walked around to the parking lot in the rear, where the white van with the green curtains was waiting for them, motor running. The lights in the museum flickered and went out as they pulled away, and Kiki noticed that the black Cadillac was the only car left in the lot. She hoped the paper bag with the broken vase was in the back of the van.

Chapter Seven

Gabrielle's farm was located about three miles out of the city on a narrow, winding back road that dipped into meadowland hollows and then swung abruptly uphill into a forested area bounded on both sides by towering pine trees. Gabrielle chattered as she drove, gesturing frequently with her hands to make a point and then grabbing the wheel again to steer around a sharp curve.

Andrew clutched the pizza box tightly throughout the whole ride and volunteered nothing to the conversation, while Kiki, scrunched in the middle, wondered how Monet and Pumpkin were faring in the back. There was a dark blue cloth hanging behind the seats, cutting off her view. The old van lurched into potholes and sent gravel scattering as Gabrielle pressed on, seemingly oblivious to the effect her driving was having on her passengers.

Finally they turned off the road into a lane marked by a country mailbox. The name Janssen was stenciled on the side of the box in peeling black paint. A cluster of buildings lay ahead. Gabrielle braked to a sudden stop in front of the main house and jumped out. Kiki and Andrew followed suit, Andrew still clutching the pizza box.

"She should be driving stock cars," Andrew muttered to Kiki while Gabrielle was letting the animals out of the back. "I think my hair turned white." He balanced the pizza box with one hand and yanked at some short strands of hair with the other, trying to pull them around so he could see better. "Tell me the truth, Kiki. Is it white?"

Kiki laughed and swatted his hand away. "Still looks brown to me," she said.

"This is it!" interrupted Gabrielle gaily. "This is the house. That building in front of the barn used to be a toolshed, but Roland fixed it up into a studio for me. Follow me! For your first visit I take you to the front door!"

At the side of the house Kiki could see a staked-off patch of land that she figured was Gabrielle's vegetable garden.

The restorer led them around and ushered them in. The old farmhouse was small and neat. Lacy curtains fluttered at the open windows, and braided rugs covered the floor.

"Don't you lock your door?" Andrew said incredulously.

Gabrielle shrugged. "Why should I? If I'm going to be robbed, they'll find a way to get in. Besides, nobody comes all the way out here . . . and I don't have anything worth stealing!"

She led them through the living room, which was furnished with old-fashioned overstuffed chairs and a sofa protected with crocheted antimacassars on the arms and on the back, just like Kiki remembered seeing at her grandmother's house. An upright piano kept watch over the room from one corner, and an ancient television set rested in another.

In the kitchen, Gabrielle switched on a light and motioned to a wooden table that sat under the window. "Put the pizza down there," she said to Andrew. "Kiki, you get some plates and napkins out, and I'll go feed Monet and his guest."

Kiki had almost forgotten about Monet's "guest." When she backtracked to look for him, she found Pumpkin on top of the piano, daintily washing up for dinner. Sprawled on the floor, but watching the cat's every move, was Monet.

"Pumpkin!" she said. "It's bad manners to sit on the furniture!"

The big cat jumped to the keyboard and walked its length twice, from high to low and low to high. Kiki could have sworn he was grinning.

"Okay, maestro," Kiki said, picking him up by the middle and plunking him down unceremoniously beside Monet, who had pulled himself to his feet and was plodding toward the kitchen.

Gabrielle led the animals out to the yard, and Kiki looked around the small kitchen. Three walls were lined with cabinets. "Which one," she said to Andrew, "has the plates?"

"Who needs plates?" he asked, stuffing what was left of a wedge of pizza in his mouth. "I'm doing just fine without one."

Kiki made a face at him. "If our hostess says get out plates, I get out plates. Logically, they should be in this one. It's closest to the table." She opened a cupboard door and quickly closed it. "Nope." She opened another. "Nope." She opened a third. "Third time's the charm!" she said, taking out three plates and setting them on the table.

"I've got the napkins under control," said Andrew, putting a napkin holder beside the plates. "Did you stumble on any glasses in the great plate search?" He went to the freezer compartment of the refrigerator and got out a tray of ice cubes.

Kiki opened another cupboard and drew in her breath. "Andrew!" she said in a soft whisper.

"And get a bowl for the ice!" he added without turning.

"Andrew!" Kiki's tone was insistent. "Look!"

He put the tray of ice down on the counter and moved toward her.

"It's the Yuan-dynasty vase! I don't believe it! I don't want to believe it!" Her voice broke as she spoke. She reached up into the cupboard and took the vase from the shelf. "Gabrielle is a thief!"

Andrew stared at the delicate vase. "Are you sure it's the real thing?" he whispered. "Maybe it's another fake. Maybe she's mass-producing them."

"No, it's the real thing," said Kiki firmly. "It feels cold, just like it did yesterday in the museum."

"You can't tell if something's genuine or fake just by how it feels," Andrew said.

"I'm sure," Kiki said, setting her jaw stubbornly. She put the vase back on the shelf and closed the cupboard door just as Gabrielle came back in from the yard.

"The animals are happy," she said. "Now we eat!"

Kiki nibbled at a piece of pizza and listened without really hearing while Gabrielle colorfully described life in Europe and Andrew talked about his aspirations to become an investigative reporter on a metropolitan daily.

"Kiki," said Gabrielle, "the pizza is too cold? I can heat it up for you."

"It isn't that," said Kiki, not looking up. She felt miserable. All she wanted to do was get home, where she didn't have to think about museums and forgeries and people who weren't what they seemed to be.

"It is something," said Gabrielle, reaching over and touching Kiki's hand. "Something is bothering you."

Kiki pushed her chair back from the table. "Yes, something is bothering me," she blurted out. She walked to the cupboard and opened the door. "*This* is bothering me!" She was close to tears as she pointed to the Chinese vase on the shelf.

Gabrielle closed her eyes and took a deep breath. "I can explain," she said. "It is not like what you think."

Monet scratched at the back door and Andrew got up from the table to let the animals in.

"Is that the real vase?" Kiki asked, the words choking in her throat.

Gabrielle nodded. "Yes. It is a complicated story."

"You were going to replace it with the fake Pumpkin broke this morning," Kiki said accusingly.

"Yes," said Gabrielle. "And I must get this vase back to the museum tonight before the curator notices it is missing. Perhaps he already has. If so, I am in trouble."

"Why did you steal it?" Kiki asked.

"I stole it," Gabrielle said, "so Ludwig Stottmeier, now Ludwig Van Kayser, could not. When he was hired by the Galliard, I knew bad things would happen to the collection," Gabrielle said. "That is why I stayed on. I explained this to you that first day I met you."

Kiki nodded.

"Ludwig works his scheme like this. He finds items in a collection that are saleable . . . things that private collectors are willing to pay for, no questions asked. He then commissions an artisan to reproduce the item, and replaces the genuine article with the forgery.

Few people, certainly not the general public, are able to tell the difference."

"But that still doesn't explain why the vase is in your cupboard," Andrew said, looking at Gabrielle.

"Yes, it does," said Kiki suddenly. "I get it! Gabrielle's beating Van Kayser to the draw! She's replacing the real articles with forgeries before he does. So what he's stealing—and selling—are really her fakes . . . reproductions that she makes!"

"That's right," said Gabrielle, nodding. "Come with me."

She held the screen door open as the two teenagers and the two pets trooped outside, and then led them along a narrow path to the converted toolshed. When they got inside, Gabrielle opened the door of a tall steel cabinet.

"These all belong to the Galliard," she said, pointing to three shelves filled with art objects. "They will all be returned when Van Kayser is relieved of his position."

Andrew drew in his breath and let out a slow whistle. "Wow," he said. "You have really been busy!"

"Can't you go to the board or to the police right now?" Kiki asked. "If these are ever found here, you could go to jail! No one would ever believe you!"

"No one believes me now, except maybe you two." She looked at Andrew and Kiki. "I must catch him in the act of stealing," she said, "or I can prove nothing."

Kiki returned her gaze. *Could you possibly be making all of this up?* she said to herself. *What if you're the bad guy and I'm an accomplice? No,* she thought, shaking her head slightly. *I'll have to go with my gut on this one.*

"Look," said Kiki, standing on tiptoe so she could see the top shelf of the cabinet. "That's the Pueblo jar that Pumpkin wanted to attack today in the American Indian exhibit!"

"The one now on exhibit is one I made," Gabrielle said. "It is a forgery. I placed it there early this morning."

"I'm beginning to think that Pumpkin has a sixth sense for picking out fakes. He didn't like the Chinese vase in the studio this morning, and he didn't like the Pueblo jar in the museum this afternoon. And he didn't like the carob chips in Mrs. Kendrick's cookies! Smart cat!"

She picked up the cat and cuddled him in her arms as she walked around the large one-room building, looking at the tools of Gabrielle's trade. There were a potter's wheel and a kiln on one side of the room, a double sink, and several easels. Supplies and half-finished projects lined the walls. Kiki stopped in front of an oil painting that looked familiar. "There's one like this hanging in the gallery!" she said.

Gabrielle nodded. "It is a copy," she said, shivering. "Let us go back to the house."

"There's one thing I don't understand," Andrew said when they were back in the kitchen. "With all the items there are in a museum, how do you know which one he's going to steal next? You could guess any one of a dozen and still be wrong."

Gabrielle nodded. "That was a problem," she said, "until I was in his office one day and noticed something on his desk." She walked over to a pile of magazines in a box by the refrigerator, picked up one, and turned to the back pages. "This is *International Collector*," she explained. "It is the trade magazine for many in the arts. Stottmeier—or Van Kayser, or whatever you want to call him—had an issue of *International Collector* on his desk and he had circled an advertisement in the back of the journal—here, like these!" She pointed to a page of small classified ads. "He was called out of the room, so I copied the ad. It was offering for sale an item like one we had here in the Galliard. I knew that because my Roland had acquired this piece when he was the curator. I was suspicious."

"So you answered the ad?" Andrew asked.

"Not directly," Gabrielle replied. "I did not want him to know I was on to him, if he had placed the advertisement. So I had a friend in Belgium, a person whose name he would not know, write to the box number."

"And it was Van Kayser selling the item?" Kiki asked, thinking that this evidence might be enough to trap the curator.

"Not quite," said Gabrielle. "He is too clever. But it is his cousin's firm, Stottmeier and Dresler, that is acting as an agent. They, of course, get a large commission."

Kiki thought for a moment and then told Gabrielle and Andrew what Elena had said to her the day before—that Dr. Van Kayser had called Gabrielle a forger and was planning to have the Board of Trustees remove her from her position. "Gabrielle, does he know that you are switching pieces? Is that why he told Elena that you were a forger?" she finished.

"I do not know for sure," she said. "He likes to—how do you say it?—put me down. And this Elena, her mother is on the board. It would serve his purposes to have me out."

"How do you do it?" Andrew asked. "Make the reproductions, I mean."

Gabrielle smiled. "There are many things I cannot reproduce. And it takes many hours. I work till very late at night," she said. "But the vases and bowls I make from molds, so I get the original shape and markings."

"Is that how you made the Chinese vase?"

"Yes, partly. But the clay would not hold in such a thin layer, so I had to reinforce it with the surgeon's cloth. Unfortunately, the coast was not clear and I could not get it into the case this morning."

Kiki looked serious. "I'm worried," she said. "If one of his buyers finds out that he's bought a forgery, Van Kayser's going to be in big trouble."

"And he's going to know it was an inside switch," Andrew added.

Gabrielle nodded. "That is why I have to get the real Chinese vase back into the collection tonight. He must not suspect what I am doing. He would not hesitate to have me arrested."

"Wait a minute," said Kiki. She got up and paced back and forth in the kitchen. Pumpkin followed at her heels.

"She's got that investigative-reporter look again," said Andrew in a teasing voice.

"Hold on!" Kiki said impatiently. She looked at Gabrielle. "He's not going to have you arrested. He couldn't risk that because he doesn't know how much you know about his scheme. You could file countercharges. I think he told Elena enough lies about you that she would discredit you with the board. He figured she'd go blab to her mother." She stopped pacing. "Actually, there are only two things he can do to stop you."

Andrew and Gabrielle stared at her.

"He could blackmail you, if he finds out that you've been taking the artifacts, or—" She paused and looked up. "Or he could steal them back and kill you in cold blood. We'd better get going," she continued. "Between the three of us, we should be able to outwit the security system."

"One moment," said Gabrielle. "First, I go alone. I cannot involve you two. You are too young for all of this. And I have an apology for you."

"For what?" Kiki asked.

Gabrielle looked down at her feet. "I am happy you and Andrew came for pizza tonight," she said. "I wanted you to come. I like you." She looked up at the teenagers, and Kiki could see tears in her eyes. "But I am using you and I do not feel good about that. I asked you to come so you could be my alibi. So I would have a reason to be in town long after the museum closed, in case someone saw my van."

"So if you're seen in town," Andrew said, "you can say you were taking us home?"

Gabrielle nodded and wiped a tear away with the back of her hand.

"Well, you are going to take us home, aren't you?" Kiki asked.

Gabrielle nodded again.

Kiki smiled. "So what's the problem? We don't want you to go alone, Gabrielle. And it's nobody's business if we go by the Galliard first. Let's go!"

Chapter Eight

"I cannot risk parking in the lot," Gabrielle said, pulling up on a side street at the back of the museum. "We must crawl through the hedge to the loading dock."

Kiki recognized where they were from her lunchtime outing with Pumpkin, who was presently sitting on her lap. Monet had been left at home to guard the farm.

Andrew, sitting beside her, was gingerly holding the Chinese vase, which Gabrielle had wrapped in a cloth and carefully packed in a box filled with Styrofoam chips.

"Before we go in," Gabrielle whispered, "I will explain the security system. Once I have unlocked the back door, I will have thirty seconds to get to the alarm box. When I have turned off the system, we then have five minutes to get to the third floor, replace the vase, and leave."

"Why just five minutes?" Andrew asked.

"It is a precaution," Gabrielle said. "If the security system is turned off for more than five minutes and no call is made to the police by an authorized person—to identify who is in the building—then they automatically send a squad car to check."

"You're not authorized to be in the building after hours?" Kiki asked.

"No," said Gabrielle. "Only the curator."

"That figures," Andrew muttered.

"Give me the flashlight," Gabrielle said. "And remember, once we are inside, five minutes is all we have. Oh, and we must take the stairs. The elevators are shut down at night. Andrew, you have a fancy watch. You will be our timekeeper. Ready?"

"Ready," said Kiki.

Gabrielle went through the hedge first and took the fragile package from Andrew so he could crawl through. Right on his heels was Kiki with the heavy cat in the crook of her arm.

The back of the museum was dark and foreboding, not at all the parklike setting that Kiki had seen at lunchtime. She glanced at the parking lot, half expecting to see the black Cadillac, but it was empty.

Gabrielle walked up the ramp to the delivery door, and Andrew and Kiki followed.

"The alarm box is on the wall to the right," she said. "Andrew, you hold the flashlight on it for me. Kiki, hold the box." Kiki put Pumpkin down and took the box from Gabrielle. She unlocked the door and they silently entered. Even Pumpkin seemed to sense the intrigue. Kiki shivered.

"All right! It's off now!" Gabrielle whispered.

Andrew checked his watch.

"Let's go!" said Gabrielle. "I will lead. I can make my way in here blindfolded." She took the flashlight from Andrew and hurried down the long hall to the rotunda and up the curving flight of stairs. Kiki looked up at the domed ceiling high above them as she passed through. There were clouds covering the moon, and no light seeped in through the glass.

They jogged up both flights of stairs. At the top Gabrielle turned sharply to the left. "In here!" she said, leading them through one room into the area with the Chinese exhibit. She passed the flashlight back to Andrew and fumbled in her pocket for her keys. The beam cast eerie shadows around them, and Kiki jumped when Pumpkin sidled alongside her and rubbed up against her leg. "Don't scare me like that!" she said to the big cat. "I almost dropped the box!"

"Two minutes thirty seconds left," Andrew said. "We'll have to go down faster than we came up!"

"Give me the vase," Gabrielle ordered. Kiki removed it from the wrappings and handed it over as Andrew scrambled to pick up the few Styrofoam chips that had fallen to the floor.

"Let's go!" Gabrielle said, locking the case.

"I'd really like to ride this banister sometime!" Kiki said, puffing, as they ran down the curving stairway and through the hall to the back door. Kiki opened the door and Andrew held the light while Gabrielle reactivated the alarm.

"Outta here!" Andrew whispered.

But just as they cleared the door, Pumpkin turned around and raced back into the museum.

"Pumpkin!"

Kiki lunged for the cat, but he was already disappearing down the dark hall. Andrew grabbed her arm.

"Now we'd really better get out of here!" he said. "He'll set off the sensors, and the place will be crawling with cops."

They scrambled into the van. Gabrielle gunned the motor and hastily drove away from the museum, but even from a safe distance of several blocks they could hear the sirens of approaching squad cars. Kiki's heart was still thudding in her chest when she got out of the van in front of her house.

"Good night, Kiki," Gabrielle said. "And *danke schön*."

Kiki nodded. "You're welcome. See you tomorrow." She ran up to the front door and let herself in.

Dr. Collier switched the sound off on the television as Kiki entered the room. "Oh," she said, "I was hoping you'd ask Mrs. Janssen to come in. I'd like to meet her."

"She was tired, Mom," Kiki said. "I'll bring her in the next time. I'm going to take a shower and wash my hair. I'll be down when I'm through."

Kiki ran up the stairs before her mother could ask any questions, and went back down only to say good night before going to bed. She was dead tired, but even after her hot shower she had trouble falling asleep. Pumpkin could look after himself, she knew, but still she worried about him.

The bedside clock-radio woke Kiki in the morning. She sat up and tried to focus her thoughts. The episode of the night before seemed like a bad dream, but she knew it had been real. She halfheartedly listened to the news as she brushed her hair, and was about to turn off the radio and go downstairs for breakfast when an item caught her full attention.

"A false alarm at the Galliard Museum last night has local authorities grinning," announced the newscaster. "Investigating officers say that a large orange cat found in the Egyptian section of the institution probably triggered the alarm, and nothing appears to be missing. Animal control officers were summoned when the cat attacked Ludwig Van Kayser, the curator, who had been called to the scene when the alarm sounded. The cat, described as hostile, escaped detention and was last seen running south on Breen Road.

"An aide to the curator, Elena Morgan, said this morning that the cat belongs to a student intern assigned to the restoration studio. As far as we know, no charges have been filed.

"And speaking of the Galliard, be sure to watch the ten o'clock news on our sister station, Channel Four, tonight for highlights of the Board of Trustees' annual dinner dance at the curator's estate on River Road. And that's the news for this half-hour."

Kiki clicked off the radio and grinned.

"Way to go, Pumpkin!" she giggled. "That's the last time I lose sleep over you!"

She was going downstairs when the phone rang. "It's for me, Mom!" she yelled. "I'll get it! . . . Hello?"

"Is this the owner of a hostile cat?" There was no mistaking Andrew's voice.

"You heard it?" Kiki said. "But it's barely eight-thirty."

"Yeah, my mother made me get up. Today I've got to clean my room."

"I thought you did that yesterday!"

"No, yesterday I ate pizza with an art thief and returned a priceless Yuan-dynasty vase to the museum."

"Shut up, Andrew!" Kiki said, giggling. "Somebody might hear you."

"Not to worry, my family won't turn me in. Besides, they've all gone to work. Hey, how do you think Elena managed to con the reporter into mentioning her name on the air?"

"You know Elena," said Kiki.

"Unfortunately I do. Well, I'm glad that Pumpkin is still selective about his enemies. Sounds like Elena and Van Kayser are running neck and neck at the top of his list." On days that Pumpkin followed Kiki to school, he usually ended up in the *Courier* office until classes were out. Elena had let her know, more than once, that she disliked Pumpkin.

At that moment there was a rustle at the kitchen door, and Kiki turned from the phone. "Speaking of said cat," she said, watching Pumpkin wriggle in through his swinging door, "here he comes now. Talk to you tonight. If I don't get it in gear, I'm going to be late."

"So be late!" Andrew said, laughing. "Tell 'em you worked overtime last night. Nah, on second thought, that may not be a good idea. Hey, maybe I'll see you this afternoon. I'm getting hooked on this culture stuff."

"Goodbye, Andrew," said Kiki. She put some food in Pumpkin's dish, and gave him fresh water, then poured herself a bowl of cereal. "I think you'd better lay low today," she said to the cat, "and catch up on your sleep. You'll be pushing your luck if you show up at the museum." Pumpkin stretched out his long body and yawned, as if he understood every word she said. "Poor baby, have a nap," she said, giving him a quick pat on the head. "Bye, Mom!" she yelled.

When Kiki walked in the front door of the museum a little after nine, Elena was in the rotunda talking to one of the guides. She was wearing a frilly white blouse and a bright red skirt with matching red sandals. She looked up as Kiki came in.

"I suppose you heard about all the trouble your stupid cat caused here last night," Elena said. "He could have broken a dozen priceless artifacts!"

"What cat?" Kiki deadpanned, without slowing her pace.

"When the radio news team came this morning, I told them who it belonged to!" Elena said, following along behind her.

"What radio news team?" Kiki said, grinning to herself as she loped down the stairs.

"Dr. Van Kayser is furious!" Elena yelled after her.

"Never heard of him," Kiki yelled back, closing the door to the restoration studio firmly behind her. She leaned up against the door and giggled. Gabrielle looked at her and grinned. "Ms. Aide-to-the-Curator is on my case already," Kiki explained.

"And Pumpkin?" Gabrielle asked. "Where is he?"

"Conked out in the kitchen at home," Kiki said. "He must have had an exciting night. He was in no shape to come to work this morning."

"He is excused," said Gabrielle, smiling. Then she turned serious. "Kiki, I thank you again for your help. Yours and Andrew's. This is getting harder and harder for me. I don't think I could have done it alone this time."

"You're welcome," Kiki said. "But Gabrielle, what bothers me is that you'll be in danger as long as Van Kayser is here. We have to figure out a way to trap him, and we have to do it quickly. I'm only going to be here a few more days, and then it's back to school."

"We will talk at our break," Gabrielle said. "And now, Collier, you will study!" She handed over a stack of magazines.

"Yes, Mrs. Janssen," Kiki said seriously. But her green eyes were dancing.

At ten-thirty they went upstairs to the cafeteria. They bought their drinks and carried them out to the veranda.

"Kiki," Gabrielle said softly, when they were settled at a table as far away from other people as they could get, "I must tell you something, and you must not show emotion, okay? While we were here last night, someone was at my farm. They were looking for the things I have . . . ah, in safekeeping."

Kiki's eyes widened. "No! Did they take anything?" she asked. "Oh, Gabrielle! That's frightening!"

The older woman shrugged. "I can find nothing missing. A few things—cups and glasses—were taken from the kitchen cupboard and left on the counter. And my bedroom closet and dresser drawers were messed up. Clothes were thrown all around."

"Did they go out to your studio?" Kiki asked.

"No, I think not. Because from the outside it looks like a toolshed, I think they decided there would be nothing of value there. Besides, Monet scared them away."

Despite the seriousness of the situation, Kiki grinned. "Monet?" she said.

"Monet is like a sleeping giant," Gabrielle said defensively. "He conserves his energy for when it is needed. He was standing guard at the front door waiting for me when I got back. His coat was covered with burrs. He took a shortcut across the field to chase their car when they left, I think."

Kiki looked up at Gabrielle and chewed on her lower lip, a nervous habit that she had when she was thinking. She frowned. "Do you want to stay at my house tonight? My mother wants to meet you anyway."

Gabrielle reached over and patted her hand. "No, but thank you," she said. "I left Monet at the house today, and tonight I need to go home and get my fancy clothes on for Dr. Van Kayser's party."

"I heard about that on the radio this morning," Kiki said.

Gabrielle looked down at her faded blue coveralls. "It is a pity. You will not get to see me in something elegant!"

"I'll watch for you on TV," Kiki said. "I'm surprised he even asked you!"

"It is an expedient move," she said. "It is a good way to shift suspicion from him. Then if something should happen to me, people will wave their hands and say, 'Oh, their feud was a thing of the past! Why, did you not see Gabrielle at his party this year?' "

"Terrific," said Kiki sarcastically.

When they left the cafeteria, Dr. Van Kayser was coming in with a man that Kiki had never seen before. The curator turned his head as he passed to avoid having to greet them. "Scuzzball," she muttered when they were out of hearing range.

Kiki read for an hour, but it was hard to concentrate on the arts when her mind was filled with fears of what might happen to Gabrielle. She just *had* to figure out some way to trap Dr. Van Kayser in the act of stealing things from the museum, and she had to do it quickly . . . before Gabrielle got hurt.

The opportunity came even sooner than she had hoped for.

Chapter Nine

"Would you do me a favor?" Gabrielle asked Kiki after lunch. She was sitting at the workbench balancing a wood carving awkwardly on one knee as she stripped away some old glue that had held it in a frame.

"Sure!" said Kiki. "Want me to hold that?"

"No," said Gabrielle. "I left my toolbox in the back of the van. Take the keys from my jacket pocket and get it for me, please. I am going to need the small chisel, but bring the whole box. It should be on the right side as you climb in the back, probably near the cloth divider."

"Okay," Kiki said, happy for the respite from reading.

There were a number of cars in the lot that day, and Kiki noticed that once again the curator had parked right beside Gabrielle's van. She tried several keys before she found the right one to unlock the back door, and when she finally did get it open, it promptly swung closed after she got inside.

"It's just not my day," Kiki said to herself, crawling down toward the front. Enough light came in through the green curtains for her to see the toolbox, wedged into the corner just where Gabrielle had said it would be. The back of the van smelled like wet dog. Kiki wrinkled her nose and grinned again at the vision of ponderous old Monet chasing off the intruders. She was crawling back to the door when she heard voices.

"You must get them tonight! She won't be home."

The curator's sharp tone wiped the grin from Kiki's face. She stayed very still. *He must be getting into his car, and someone's with him,* she thought.

"You were fools to go there last night! She could have seen you and called the police."

He's talking about Gabrielle! They're going to search her place again tonight . . . while she's at the party at Van Kayser's.

Another man said something, but Kiki couldn't make out his words. *He must be on the other side of the car,* she thought, *or getting into one of the other cars*. There was silence, and Kiki waited for the sound of a motor, but none came.

Suddenly, the second voice was right under the window of the van. "You listen to me, Ludwig!" The tone was threatening. "She's figured out your little scheme, and if you go down, we all go down. I've got a buyer flying into New York on Saturday, and I expect to have that cat there, crated and ready. Understand? And since you won't get it out, I'll have to do it myself!"

Cat? What cat? thought Kiki. For a moment, a mental picture of Pumpkin, crated and ready to be loaded on a plane, crossed her mind. If the situation hadn't been so serious, she might have laughed. What cat were they talking about?

"The cat is not something I can slip under my suit jacket and walk out with," Van Kayser replied sarcastically. "And you'll have to get the replica in!"

"And the jewelry?"

"Somewhat easier. But there's a timing problem. There's a university study group coming in Friday afternoon. They'll be there until closing time. The professor is very knowledgable. He lived in Egypt for seventeen years. He'd know in a minute. Those items must not be moved until after that class leaves."

"Well, I'm not planning to come in in day-light!"

"I'm glad to hear that. I'll leave the key to the exhibit case with my intern. You under-stand the alarm system?"

"Yes."

"And you have the key to the delivery en-trance?"

"Yes."

"I will make the call to the police at nine o'clock from the beach house. Take care of the dog."

A car door slammed. "Don't mess up to-night, Dresler. You do your part, I'll do mine. By Saturday morning, Mrs. Janssen will be history around here."

"Unless the *udjat* eye really works," said the other man.

"What are you talking about?" scoffed Van Kayser.

"She carries one with her at all times. Her husband gave it to her—he told me about it years ago."

The roar of the car engine drowned out Van Kayser's reply.

Kiki sat on the floor of the van, holding the toolbox tightly in her hands, until she heard the other car motor start. When she was sure both had left the parking lot, she opened the back door of the van and got out. Her legs were unsteady as she walked back into the museum. When she got back down to the lab, Gabrielle looked up at her questioningly.

"I . . . I stopped at the ladies' room on my way back," she said, hoping that would explain the elapsed time. It seemed as if she had been in the van forever. Should she tell Gabrielle, or shouldn't she? She didn't want Gabrielle to panic, and she thought she should be able to come up with a plan to foil the curator's plot. But she couldn't seem to come up with a good idea.

She worried about it until it was time to meet Andrew upstairs for their daily exhibit tour. "Can we get something to drink before we do the collection?" Kiki asked Gabrielle.

"Certainly. But there is something bothering you. I can see it in your eyes."

"Yes," said Kiki. "I need to talk to both you and Andrew."

They gave up their special place on the veranda in favor of a corner table. A strong wind had come up, discouraging anyone from sitting outside.

"Now, Kiki, what is troubling you?" Gabrielle asked.

"When I went to get your toolchest after lunch, I overheard Dr. Van Kayser talking to someone. He didn't know I was there. Gabrielle . . . they're going back to your place tonight to look for the things again!"

"Ah," said Gabrielle. "Monet will be busy."

"Gabrielle, they know you're not going to be there!" Suddenly Kiki had an idea. "Let me and Andrew go out there with you after work. We can stay until you get back from the party, and then you can bring us home."

"Absolutely not," Gabrielle said. "I will not permit it."

"But Gabrielle! You can't call the police to protect you until . . . until the museum pieces are back in the museum. Just let us go and watch the place."

"No. Thank you, but no. The subject is closed. I will get some more coffee. You would like some more soda?"

"No, thanks," Kiki said.

"Some more ice, please," Andrew said, handing her his cup. When Gabrielle was a safe distance away from the table, he turned to Kiki. "Wow, when you eavesdrop, you don't mess around. It's big-time!"

"Andrew, that's not all." Keeping an eye on Gabrielle as she went through the line, Kiki quickly told him the rest of the conversation she had overheard. "Somebody's got to be there tonight," she said, "whether she likes it or not. This time they'll be expecting Monet. They'll come prepared. They may hurt him . . . or something worse." She leaned forward. "Andrew, how do you feel about being a stowaway?"

" 'Scuse me?" he said.

Kiki slipped Gabrielle's keys out of her pocket. "I still have her van keys. We can unlock the door now and hide in the back later. She'll never know. When she goes into the house to change into her party clothes, we get out and hide. She leaves, and we're there!"

"Tricky," said Andrew. "But it might work. What do we tell our parents?"

Kiki grinned.

"Oh," said Andrew, nodding his head. "You're at my house and I'm at your house. You know, one of these times we're going to get caught on that one."

"Well, Mom's working tonight anyhow, so I'll be telling the answering machine," Kiki said. "Here! Take the keys and go unlock the back door. I'll keep her talking."

Kiki watched Andrew grin sheepishly at Gabrielle as he passed her coming back with the ice and the coffee.

"Little boys' room," Kiki explained when Gabrielle sat down. She reached for the cup of ice, fished a piece out with her fingers, and crunched on it.

When Andrew came back he slipped Kiki the keys under the table. Gabrielle gave them an abbreviated tour of the American Indian section, and when Andrew left, she and Kiki went back downstairs. "It has been a strange day," Gabrielle said. "I think we will close up a little early. Then I can get home and get cleaned up for Dr. Van Kayser's gala party!" There was an overtone of sarcasm in her voice.

"Sure," Kiki said. "Have a good time tonight. Oh, here are your keys, Gabrielle." She pulled the keys from her pocket and put them on the workbench. "See you tomorrow!"

Gabrielle gave her a hug as she was leaving. "Thank you for your offer, Kiki," she said. "But I cannot have you and Andrew in danger for my sake. You understand?"

"I guess," said Kiki. She closed the studio door and ran up the stairs to the main floor, out the front door, and around to the parking lot. Andrew was waiting in the back of the van, and Pumpkin was with him.

"Where did he come from?" Kiki asked, crawling in and pulling the door shut behind her as her pet licked at her face.

"He was waiting in the lot when I got here,"

Andrew said. "I guess he just can't bear to stay away from that piano."

"Oh, spare me," said Kiki.

Ten minutes elapsed before Gabrielle came out and started the motor. The van lurched forward, and Andrew slapped his hand against his forehead. "I don't know what's worse," he whispered, "sitting back here not knowing when she's running off the road, or being up there and seeing it all unfold before your eyes."

Kiki giggled appreciatively, remembering the previous night's ride with the pizza. "When we get there, you get out first and take Pumpkin—I hadn't planned on him—and then I'll get out. We can hide at the side of the house until she leaves."

"Right."

Everything went exactly as planned, except for Pumpkin. He resisted all efforts to keep him restrained, and from the inside of the house they could hear Monet making plaintive little cries, as if he knew his friend was on the property.

"She didn't leave a minute too soon," Kiki said as Gabrielle drove down the lane toward the road. "I couldn't have held him for another minute!"

Pumpkin ran to the door and scratched on

the screen for admittance. On the other side, Kiki could hear Monet scratching as well, and when she opened the door, it was as if the two of them had not seen each other for months—licking and sniffing and making animal welcoming noises. Greetings completed, Pumpkin leaped to the top of the piano and washed up for dinner, while Monet sank in his usual shapeless heap on the floor with an audible sigh.

"Okay, chief, what now?" Andrew asked. "Do we go out and keep watch at the toolshed, or what?"

"I don't think they'll come until after dark," Kiki replied. "Which will give us enough time to get the stuff moved from out there to in here."

"Good thinking. Since they've already checked the house," Andrew said, "they won't be looking in here again."

"Right. Let's go!"

On the way out, Kiki quickly checked to see that there was food and water out for the pets, and then she and Andrew ran down the path to Gabrielle's studio. Like the house, it was unlocked.

One by one, the teenagers removed the treasures from the metal cabinet and carried them to the house, hiding each one in an unlikely place—the flour canister, a shoe box, a clothes hamper—until every precious museum piece they could find had been hidden in the dwelling.

"Piece of cake!" said Andrew, dusting off his hands. He looked out the window. "It's getting dark. Do you have the flashlight?"

Kiki nodded. "We may have a long wait," she said, "but we don't dare turn on the lights in here. They know that Gabrielle's at Van Kayser's. They'd suspect something if they saw a light. Is there anything to eat?"

Andrew checked the refrigerator. "Some leftover pizza and a couple of chicken legs. And a bowl of oranges if you want your vitamin C for the day."

"Any of it! All of it! I'm starved," said Kiki. Just then there was a strange noise. "I wish that wind would stop. It's spooky." The old farmhouse creaked and groaned with each gust, and eerie whistling noises came from the attic.

Andrew brought the food over and they sat at the table and munched, watching for signs of a car on the lane leading to the house. Several went by on the main road, but none turned in.

"We could play twenty questions," said Kiki. The wind and the waiting were beginning to get on her nerves. A sudden, smashing chord from the piano made Kiki jump. She peered into the other room, where Pumpkin was walking haughtily up and down the keys. He spied her and ran over, jumping into her lap. "I wish I'd brought a deck of cards," she said, turning her attention back to Andrew.

Kiki and Andrew read for a while, then played guessing games with states and trees and flowers and birds and song titles until they both were bored silly. Occasionally, Pumpkin would wander into the living room and give one of his mini-concerts, but for the most part, the animals slept curled up together under the kitchen table.

Soon it was too dark to read. They couldn't watch TV, since even the light from the television screen might tip their expected visitors that someone was in the house.

"We could tell ghost stories," said Andrew, teasing Kiki as she fidgeted.

"I'll pass," she said. "The thing that bothers me most about today is what that guy said about the *udjat* eye."

"What is the *udjat* eye?"

"It's a symbol the Egyptians put on jewelry. They thought it could make sick people well or bring someone back from the dead.

Gabrielle has one on a ring that her husband gave her."

"Gabrielle's not sick," Andrew said dourly.

"Not funny, Andrew," Kiki said. "That's the scary part. I think they're really planning to kill her. But they can't afford to until they find the things from the museum that she's got hidden out here."

"You think they're going to hit the Egyptian exhibit next?" he asked. "The jewelry?"

Kiki nodded. "And I think they were talking about the ebony cat. I didn't tell Gabrielle everything I heard. I probably should have. I guess I will tomorrow. What time is it?"

"Eight-forty."

She leaned closer to the window and moved the curtain aside a little. "That's funny. I thought I saw a car coming over that hill a minute ago, but it hasn't come up out of the hollow."

As she spoke Monet struggled to his feet with a guttural, threatening growl.

"They're here," said Andrew grimly, stopping in the middle of peeling an orange. "I can see the outline of the vehicle over there by the barn. It looks like a Jeep. They must have turned off their lights and cut across the field."

Monet growled again and Andrew leaned

over to pat him, but the dog ignored his hand and stalked to the door. Pumpkin, sensing the other animal's anxiety, jumped off Kiki's lap and joined Monet at the door.

Soon they could detect the beam from a flashlight coming from behind the barn, aimed toward the toolshed.

"They're going inside!" Kiki whispered.

Monet growled again.

"It's okay, fellow. They're not coming up here tonight."

The door creaked and Kiki jumped.

"Where's Pumpkin?" she said out loud.

But before the words left her mouth, she knew where he was. They had left the inside door ajar just enough for him to wedge his fat body between it and the screen. Kiki ran to the door, but she was not in time. With a yowl that would raise the dead, he booted the screen door open and raced out into the night with Monet flying at his heels—both of them headed straight for the toolshed. Monet's frantic barking alerted the people inside. They scrambled out through the door as the animals attacked in tandem and the teenagers ran down the path.

"Shoot him!" one of them yelled. A woman's voice!

There was a sharp crack and a flash of light,

and then a scream and a thud. Kiki could see the woman fall to the ground. She rolled over and thrashed out with her hands. As Kiki got closer, she realized that Pumpkin was clawing at the woman's face. Monet staggered and then, with a surge of energy, started to run again. The man with the gun turned, raised his arm, and aimed at the dog. But before he could get off another shot, the gun was knocked from his hand. Kiki turned just in time to see Andrew fire off a second orange!

The woman on the ground threw Pumpkin aside and jumped to her feet, holding her face. They both ran behind the barn toward the Jeep, with the outraged orange cat and Andrew in hot pursuit.

"Monet!" Kiki yelled, tears rolling down her cheeks. She dropped to her knees beside the dog, who whimpered and licked at her hand as he lay on the hard ground, bleeding from the gunshot wound. When the Jeep's motor started he woofed once and raised his head, as if he weren't through with the chase, but he didn't have enough strength to get up.

"Andrew!" Kiki yelled. "Come here! Hurry!" She kicked off her tennis shoe and took off her sock. The bullet had torn into the fleshy part of his back leg, exiting on his rump, and the more he moved, the more he bled. She had to stop the bleeding, she knew that. Monet cried out again, and she stroked his floppy ears with one hand and wiped her own tears away with the back of the other. "We'll get you inside, fellow," she said, "but first I've got to stop the bleeding. You're not going to like this." She knotted her sock, balled it up, and pressed the cloth into the wound. The dog flinched and whined piteously.

Pumpkin ambled up, surveyed the situation, and started washing Monet's face with great sweeping, sympathetic licks of his pink tongue. Andrew, close behind him, knelt down beside Kiki and the dog. "They're gone," he said. "How bad is it?"

"I don't know," Kiki answered, sniffing. "He's lost a lot of blood. We have to get him inside. I can't see out here."

Andrew jumped up and ran. "There's a piece of plywood over here against the toolshed," he yelled over his shoulder.

Using the plywood as a stretcher, they carried Monet into the kitchen and put him on the table. Pumpkin made comforting noises by his ear while Kiki examined the wound. The pressure had stopped the bleeding, and she decided not to try to clean the area in case the disturbance would start it up again.

"See if you can find a blanket," Kiki said to Andrew.

He was back almost immediately with an afghan. She was tucking it around the wounded animal when she saw something unusual about the dog. "Andrew! Monet has an *udjat* eye tooled into his leather collar!"

"I hope it works for him," Andrew muttered as he studied a card hanging by the phone. "Just for insurance, I'm calling a vet. Gabrielle must have a vet! . . . There it is—Gregory Locker, D.V.M."

He dialed and Kiki listened as he talked to the vet's answering service. His voice squeaked a little as he talked, and Kiki knew he was feeling the same nervous jitters that she was.

"Well, no, we can't bring him in. Okay. We'll wait for the call. Do you have any idea how long it will be? . . . Okay. Thanks."

He turned to Kiki. "They're going to page Dr. Locker. He's out in this area somewhere with a sick horse. How's Monet doing?"

"Okay, I think."

"I'm impressed," Andrew said, coming over to the table. "I never would have thought to stuff a sock in there to stop the bleeding. Where did you learn to do that? Your mom?"

"Mostly. And from a Red Cross course I took. I guess if you live around medicine all your life, you pick up things. Mom told me about stopping somebody's bleeding once by sticking her fist in the wound until they could get the gauze packs. Anyway, I think Monet's lucky the bullet went on through."

"Are you going to be a doctor?"

"I don't know." She giggled nervously, feeling a giddy kind of relief now that the vet was on his way and the intruders were gone. "Are you going to be a major-league pitcher? If it hadn't been for you, Monet would be dead. That guy was aiming at his head."

Andrew rolled his eyes. "Actually," he said, "that was my secret orange rocket pitch. Outlawed in all major-league parks, you know."

"Well, I don't ever want you pitching things at me," Kiki said. "You knocked the gun right out of his hand."

Andrew nodded. "I put it on the piano," he said. "The gun, that is."

"You'd better find another spot," Kiki told him, eyeing Pumpkin. "The piano's Pumpkin's hangout. He did a good job tonight, too!"

"Fantastic! He took care of the woman in nothing flat!" Andrew picked up the weapon.

"Where will this be safe from our heroic cat?" Without waiting for an answer, he muttered, "Almost no place." He finally opened the refrigerator door and put the gun in the vegetable crisper. "He doesn't like lettuce, does he?"

"Not his first choice," Kiki said, smiling.

The phone rang, and Andrew grabbed it on the first ring.

"What did he say?" Kiki asked anxiously when he finished talking to the vet. "About the gunshot wound?"

"Well, first he asked if the bleeding had stopped, and then he said to keep the dog warm. He told me Gabrielle's is right on his way back to town. He'll be here in half an hour or so. And then mumbled something about stupid hunters wandering around after dark."

"Gabrielle may be here by the time he arrives," Kiki said. "What time is it?"

"Almost ten."

"I'd better call home and leave another message," Kiki said. "Mom's working three to eleven, but she still may get home before I do. I'm just going to tell her we came out here. No details."

"Yeah, me too," said Andrew, "except I'm not going to talk to an answering machine. With luck, I'll get one of my brothers."

They made their calls, checked on Monet again, and sat back to wait for the vet.

"Let's watch the news," Kiki suggested. "Channel Four was going to cover the party."

Andrew turned on the TV in the living room and shoved the set around to face the doorway so they could stay with Monet and watch from the kitchen.

Coverage of the party came on just before the weather.

"Earlier this evening," said the announcer, "our Channel Four crew visited the home of Ludwig Van Kayser, curator of the Galliard Museum, where the institution's annual dinner dance was in progress."

The TV crew interviewed Dr. Van Kayser and one of the board members and then they showed some clips of the dance, which had been held in the ballroom of his estate.

"Some pad," said Andrew. "Look! There's Gabrielle!"

"She's dancing with Dr. Allenby!" Kiki said excitedly. "He's my doctor! And look at that dress she's got on!"

"Sure is a darn sight cuter than coveralls," said Andrew, faking an old man's quavery voice.

Gabrielle had worn a long-sleeved, high-necked gold dress shimmering with sequins.

130

As they danced she was talking to the doctor, who smiled and nodded his head.

"Look!" Andrew shouted. "Over there in the corner. Upper right!" He pointed at the screen. "It's Ms. Artifact of the Year! Oh, we'll be hearing about this for a while!"

Kiki looked to where he was pointing. Elena, wearing a jade-green sheath, was standing by a marble statue, animatedly talking to a blond man in a tuxedo.

"That'll be her next column," Kiki predicted, making a face at the screen. " 'How the Beautiful People Live.' I wonder how she got invited?"

"Her mother's on the board," said Andrew. "How else?"

The lights of a vehicle swept by the kitchen window, and Kiki pulled aside the curtain. "It's the van!" she said. "Gabrielle's home!" Andrew switched on the outside light and opened the door. "It's just us, Gabrielle!" he yelled, stepping out where she could see him.

"You children!" she scolded, hurrying up the walk. "I told you I didn't want you here!" She came into the kitchen and stopped, staring at the dog lying on the table. *Monet!*

"He's okay, I think," Kiki said. "Dr. Locker's coming."

Gabrielle rushed over to Monet. They

barely had time to explain what had happened before the vet's truck pulled into the yard.

"He thinks it was hunters out after dark," Andrew said. "I didn't correct him."

"Good!" said Gabrielle.

When Dr. Locker had finished treating Monet, he offered Kiki and Andrew a ride back to town. "He'll be good as new in a couple of weeks," he reassured Gabrielle. "It was a flesh wound." He smiled at Kiki. "You were lucky to have this little lady around. He could have bled to death."

Gabrielle arched one eyebrow and tried to look stern. "I am lucky to have these uninvited guests?" she said. And then she gave both Kiki and Andrew a hug. "I will see you tomorrow. Thank you very, very much."

She grabbed Pumpkin and hugged him too, her eyes glistening with emotion. "And you too, Pumpkin!"

Chapter Ten

"How's Monet?" Kiki asked Gabrielle the next morning when she got to the museum. She put her backpack down on the floor, and Pumpkin walked out and went directly to Monet's empty blanket.

"He is much better. He slept most of the night with the medicine the doctor gave him. I will work just half a day today so I can go home to be with him."

"I'm glad he's better," Kiki said.

Meeeooow. Pumpkin sat erect on the blanket and cocked his head, looking at Gabrielle, who came over and gave him a chocolate chip from a bag on the workbench. "You see, I now keep your treats handy, Pumpkin," she said, stroking his fur. "You are a brave pussycat to save my Monet."

Eeoow! Pumpkin closed his eyes and sighed in obvious enjoyment as he squished the candy around in his mouth.

Kiki and Gabrielle laughed. "He's such a ham," said Kiki.

"I thank you again," Gabrielle said seriously to Kiki. "You and Andrew. If you had not been there, Monet would be dead. I hope your mother was not too angry with your lateness."

"No, I beat her home by half an hour," Kiki said, smiling impishly. "And I didn't want her to worry, so I didn't tell her what happened, or why Andrew and I were at your place. She really wants to meet you, Gabrielle. Maybe some night—when Monet's better—you could come and have dinner with us?"

"I would like that."

Kiki took a breath. "Gabrielle, I didn't tell you everything I overheard yesterday, when I was in the van."

Gabrielle took off her dusty glasses and wiped them on the front of her coveralls. "It is not good, yes?"

"Right." Kiki hesitated, weighing the pros and cons of telling Gabrielle the whole conversation with its implications, or just telling her the facts. "Van Kayser and his people are planning to steal something else from the museum. Tomorrow night."

Gabrielle held up her hand to stop Kiki from saying anything more. "It is happening that soon, then," she said dejectedly. "I will not have time to reproduce it."

"You know about it?"

Gabrielle nodded. "It is in the Egyptian collection, yes? They will take the ebony cat."

Kiki looked surprised. "How did you know?"

"There was another ad in the journal," Gabrielle explained. "They are getting bolder. The cat is the largest item they have yet tried to remove."

"Tomorrow night Van Kayser will call the police at nine o'clock from his beach house, to okay the security system being turned off. But it's not just the cat they're after. They're going to take the jewelry, too. The *udjat* eye pieces."

Gabrielle sank down on the stool. "No! No! They were Roland's prize acquisitions! I cannot let him do that. . . . I am so weary of all this," she said, close to tears. "This cat-and-mouse game that Van Kayser plays. He takes the very best objects from the collection, moves on, changes his name, and goes unstopped. Because of him, I have become a thief." She stood up, her chin jutting out and her back straight. "I am through," she said. "I will play his game no more. Tomorrow I will bring the artifacts back and call the authorities."

Kiki moved close and put her arm around her. "It's probably best," she said. "Surely they won't prosecute you for trying to protect the Galliard collection! Andrew and I can tell them why you did what you did."

Gabrielle shrugged. "I am a forger and a thief. It matters not what my motivation was. And now," she said abruptly, "we must get to today's work. I need information on this painting before I can repair its damage. You will go, please, to the curator's office and get the card on it. It is item number five-one-two-two."

"Yes, of course," said Kiki, glad for the chance to get out of the studio for a few minutes. She walked up the stairs all the way to the third floor to stretch her legs and give herself a little time to think. Maybe Gabrielle was right. Maybe the justice system didn't look at the motivation behind a crime. But it didn't seem fair.

Elena answered her knock at the curator's office door.

"Yes?" she asked.

"Elena, I need the card on item number five-one-two-two," Kiki said. "An oil painting. Seventeenth century."

"I told you before, you can't take the cards from this office," Elena said in her imperious voice.

"Just get me the card and I'll copy the information," Kiki said, walking past her into the office. "I don't want to take your precious cards out of the office."

"Did you happen to watch Channel Four last night?" Elena asked, unexpectedly becoming friendly.

Kiki made a face behind the other girl's back. "I watched it," Kiki said, wandering around the office while Elena disappeared into the file room. She sat on the corner of the curator's desk and picked up a carved ivory letter opener.

"Did you see me? Did you see the man I was with?" Elena's voice was muffled. The file room was barely more than a large closet, and her back was to Kiki.

"Yes, I saw you," Kiki said. "You had on a green dress." While she talked, Kiki was looking at some papers on Van Kayser's desk. She laid the letter opener down on top of the papers and was about to go to the door of the file room when she saw it: a silver key on a chain, lying on top of a piece of notepaper that said *Dresler will pick up*.

"What's the number?" Elena called out.

"Uh . . . five-two-one-one—no, five-one-two-two!"

Kiki's mind was reprocessing the conversation she had overheard while in the van. *This must be the key to the* udjat *eye display case*! She shoved her hand in her jeans pocket and pulled out her keychain. Three keys: bicycle lock, school locker, and front door. The bicycle-lock key resembled it most closely. She took it off her chain and quickly made the switch just as Elena came out of the room with the card.

"Did you see the man I was with?" she repeated. Kiki pretended to be very interested in a piece of modern art hanging over the credenza. She shoved the display-case key deep down in her pocket.

"The big handsome blond guy?"

"Yes!" said Elena, pleased that Kiki had noticed. "Troy's an art dealer from Los Angeles," she continued. "He sat by me at dinner, too. It was a wonderful party. I almost didn't come to work today, I was so tired . . . except I knew that Dr. Van Kayser was only going to be here briefly this morning. He's taking some friends to his beach house at Deer Lake, and I promised him I'd keep the office open. He has a European dealer coming by to pick up something important."

Kiki bit the corners of her mouth to keep from grinning. *Something important—like the key to my bike lock*, she thought. She took the card from Elena, copied the information, and handed it back to her.

"Thanks," Kiki said. As she walked out the door she could feel the key in her jeans pocket. *It may not stop them tomorrow night*, she thought with a grim smile, *but it will slow them down*.

Gabrielle was very quiet when she got back to the studio. Kiki gave her the information from the card and settled down to read some more journals. She didn't find them as boring now as she had when she'd started on Monday. Had that been just four days earlier? She was surprised at how much she had learned just from studying in the mornings and taking tours with Gabrielle in the afternoons. And each day, Gabrielle had let her assist with some hands-on work in the studio.

They skipped their usual morning break, and at eleven o'clock Gabrielle cleaned off the workbench. "I will go home for the day now," she said to Kiki. "I am worried about Monet. But I'll be in early tomorrow. There is much to be done." She took a key from a nail over the door. "This is a key to the studio," she said, handing it to Kiki. "You may leave at noon, if you like. Lock the door when you leave. I will see you tomorrow."

Kiki finished the article she was reading and then went upstairs and wandered through two of the main-floor exhibit rooms. On an impulse, she climbed the stairs to the second floor and went into the Egyptian room. A group of children were in there with two parents guiding them, and the unnaturally hushed voices of the children reinforced Kiki's feeling that this exhibit cast a mysterious spell over all its visitors.

She walked past the sarcophagus and the ebony cat, and over to the case that held the *udjat* eye jewelry. The heavy gold necklace and matching bracelet were intricately engraved with the eye and set with precious stones.

"It's looking at me," said a small voice at her elbow. A little girl was standing there, staring at the jewelry.

"I know," said Kiki. "That's called an *udjat* eye. The Egyptians believed that it could make sick people better." The group gathered around Kiki as she explained. "Some thought it was so powerful that it could bring dead people back to life."

"It's spooky," said the little girl.

"Do you think so?" said Kiki.

The group moved on, and Kiki went downstairs to collect Pumpkin. She locked up the studio and pocketed the key.

When she got home she called Andrew.

"No tour today," she told him. "Gabrielle went home early to be with Monet. She says he's doing okay."

"How's Gabrielle?"

"Not so hot. She knew before I told her that they were going after the ebony cat. It was in one of the ads. And when I told her about the jewelry, she said she was through playing their games. She's going to bring everything back tomorrow and call the police."

"Turn herself in?" Andrew let out a breathy whistle.

"I guess so. So if you have any brilliant ideas between now and tomorrow, call me."

"Right. Talk to you later."

Kiki was fixing a peanut-butter-and-jelly sandwich when the phone rang.

"Hi, Kiki. I thought I'd be talking to your machine. How come you're not at the museum today?"

"Hi, Mrs. Kendrick. Well, I was there this morning, but Mrs. Janssen went home early, so I came home, too."

"Lucky for me! I know this is short notice,

but would you be able to sit with Jeffrey tonight? We'll be home by nine."

"Sure," Kiki said. "What time?"

"Is six too early? We're meeting some friends for dinner."

"That's okay," Kiki said. "See you at six."

When Kiki arrived at the Kendricks', Jeffrey was just finishing his dinner.

"Pumpkin!" he yelled, sliding down off the chair and reaching for the cat. Pumpkin evaded him by jumping up on the table and licking up the remains of Jeffrey's meal.

"Pumpkin!" Kiki said, grabbing him around the middle and plopping him down on the floor. "Mind your manners!"

Mrs. Kendrick laughed. "I have some real chocolate chip cookies for him this time," she said, handing Jeffrey two cookies—one for him and one for the cat. "No carob chips."

"He doesn't deserve anything, acting like that," Kiki said. "Did you go to the Galliard party last night?"

"Yes, it was lovely."

"It was stuffy and boring," said Mr. Kendrick, coming into the kitchen. "Those arty types are more snooty than lawyers."

Mrs. Kendrick ignored him and looked at Kiki apologetically. "We didn't call you to sit because my sister was here. She stayed with Jeffrey."

"That's okay," Kiki said. "That wasn't why I asked. I saw some of it on TV, but I didn't see you."

"That's because I found a potted palm to hide behind when I saw those cameras come in," Mr. Kendrick said, reaching for a cookie. "There's hope for next year, though. I hear that the curator has a beach house out on Deer Lake. I'm going to propose that all the spouses of the trustees bring hiking boots or fishing tackle or bathing suits. The trustees can all dress up and dance with the dealers or each other while those of us without culture are out catching the entrée or working up a real appetite."

"Oh, Lorne!" said Mrs. Kendrick.

Kiki grinned. She enjoyed hearing Mr. Kendrick tease his wife. When she first sat for them, she had been in awe of the county's new district attorney, but she quickly learned that he was good-natured and kind.

"How are you enjoying your week with Mrs. Janssen?" Mrs. Kendrick asked.

"It's fun," Kiki said. "Different from what I expected. But then, I didn't really know *what* to expect."

Certainly not an international art-theft ring

or a restorer who forges art objects and steals real ones, she thought.

"Dr. Allenby tells me that Mrs. Janssen is an artist in her own right," Mrs. Kendrick said. "He says she lives on a farm outside of town, and she has a whole barn full of paintings and sculpture that she's done over the years."

Kiki gulped. "I didn't know that," she said, picturing the old barn behind the toolshed, and wondering if it really was full of artwork.

"I guess she just stopped painting when her husband got ill. And when he died, Dr. Allenby said she lost all interest in her artwork."

"Let's go, Susan!" Mr. Kendrick said, tugging on his wife's arm. "Or we'll get there just in time for dessert. And I might be too full for that," he added, swiping another cookie from the plate on the table.

"We'll be home around nine," Mrs. Kendrick said as they left.

"No rush," said Kiki. "No school tomorrow, and I don't have any big plans."

She didn't know it at the time, but the next day was going to be one of the biggest days in her life.

Chapter Eleven

Kiki arrived at the Galliard the next morning in a bad mood. When she was walking home from the Kendricks' the night before, Pumpkin had picked a fight with a stray cat, confronted a poodle being walked by a neighbor, and then run off. The neighbor had called her mother to complain, and on top of that, Dr. Allenby had told her mother at work the previous afternoon about the Galliard dinner dance at the curator's, and how Mrs. Janssen had raved to him about having Kiki as an intern for the week.

Which had led Dr. Collier to ask Kiki to explain why she'd been at Mrs. Janssen's when Mrs. Janssen was at Dr. Van Kayser's. Kiki's lame explanation that she had been sitting for Gabrielle's sick dog didn't have a lot of credibility, and her mother had decided that unless she could come up with a better reason, she could spend the weekend at home. In other words, when Kiki finished her day at the museum, she was grounded.

Pumpkin, being an intelligent and perceptive animal, hadn't returned home to face the music.

Kiki went down the stairs to the restoration studio and turned the knob. The door was locked. That was strange. Gabrielle had said she'd be in early that morning. Was Monet worse? Maybe he'd developed an infection in the wound.

Kiki took the studio key from her pocket and unlocked the door. She switched on the light over the workbench where she kept her stack of periodicals. She'd decided the night before that she was going to check through all of them to see if there were any articles about Egyptian artifacts.

But the journals were not on the corner of the workbench, where she had left them. Kiki frowned. She was positive she had left them there. She remembered the rich gold and maroon colors on the cover of the issue on top. She bent down. The pile of magazines was now under the bench. Puzzled, Kiki picked them up and settled herself on the stool to read. But she had trouble concentrating. As far as she knew, there were only three keys to the studio—Gabrielle's, the extra one that

Kiki had, and the curator's, but he was at Deer Lake. Gabrielle wouldn't have come back yesterday. She was too worried about Monet. Kiki slipped off the stool and walked around the room. Nothing seemed to be missing, and nothing else seemed to be disturbed.

There was a knock at the door.

"Coming," Kiki said as she walked over to open it.

Elena stood in the hall outside.

"So this is where you've been hiding all week," Elena said, pushing the door farther open and looking around. "It's messy in here." She entered without being invited and walked the length of the room, ignoring Kiki, peering into corners like a real-estate agent looking at an unsuitable piece of property. "How can you stand the smell?" she asked, wrinkling her nose.

"I don't smell anything," Kiki said, realizing that she must have become so used to the turpentine odor that she didn't notice it anymore. "What do you want?"

"I'm here to deliver a message," Elena said. "Mrs. Janssen won't be in today. Her brother is seriously ill in Pennsylvania. She left on an early-morning flight." She walked back to the door, and Kiki half expected her to take out a tissue to protect her hand as she touched the knob. "You can go home."

"Wait a minute," Kiki said, a question in her tone. But Elena was already climbing the stairs.

She started after her but thought better of it. Instead, she closed the studio door and sat down, journals forgotten. She needed some thinking time. Gabrielle had never mentioned a brother, and Kiki had assumed that any family she had was in Europe. And where was Monet if Gabrielle was on a plane? Had she boarded him at Dr. Locker's? Was this story some concoction of Elena's?

Elena was a pain, but Kiki didn't think she'd tell an outright lie. Kiki's sixth sense was nagging at her. Despite his personality imperfections, she wished Pumpkin were there. It helped to have him to talk to when she was dissecting her way through some problem.

Had Gabrielle talked to Elena? That wasn't exactly what Elena had said. She'd said, "I'm here to deliver a message." So where did the message come from?

Kiki locked the studio and ran up the stairs to the pay phone on the first floor. She fished in her pocket for some change and dialed Gabrielle's number. Busy. If Gabrielle was already on her way to Pennsylvania, who was using her phone? Of course, it could be another incoming call dialed at the same time, but that was unlikely. Kiki's heart started to thump. Something was wrong. She could feel it.

She got on the elevator and rode to the third floor.

"Elena!" she said, marching into the curator's office without knocking. "When did Gabrielle call?"

Elena was curled up in one of the easy chairs by the coffee table, reading a fashion magazine. She jumped as Kiki came in, and hastily put the magazine on the table, cover side down.

"Don't come barging in here like that!" she said, standing up. "Dr. Van Kayser could be in an important meeting!"

"Well, I doubt it, since he's out of town," Kiki said. "When did Gabrielle call?"

"Gabrielle did not call," Elena explained patiently, as if to a small child. "Dr. Van Kayser called me this morning from his beach house—"

That was all Kiki needed to hear. She hurried out the door and raced down the stairs, taking them two and three at a time. When she reached the main floor she went directly to the pay phone.

Gabrielle's line was still busy. That cinched it. Something was wrong. Kiki dialed the Carlisles' number, and Andrew answered.

"Want to go for a bike ride?" she asked. She hurriedly explained the situation. "I don't think she has a brother in Pennsylvania. I think Van Kayser may have her at his beach house on Deer Lake. I'll catch the next bus, and you meet me at my house in twenty minutes."

"I'll be there!"

Kiki ran back downstairs, locked the studio and left. When she got home, Andrew was waiting on the front porch, his bike leaning up against the garage. Five minutes later, the two teenagers were on the road leading to Gabrielle's farm.

"This is almost as good as the bike trail," Andrew yelled back over his shoulder. "No traffic!"

When they turned off into the lane that led to the farm, Kiki braked. Andrew circled around and skidded to a stop beside her. "What?" he asked, following her gaze.

"Andrew, the van," she said through tight lips. "The van is there. It's parked right where she usually leaves it. If she did go to Pennsylvania, how did she get to the airport?"

"Maybe a neighbor took her. Don't jump to

150

conclusions." He kicked the pedal forward and rode slowly down the dirt lane, Kiki close behind.

The house was unusually quiet. There were no sounds—no birds chirping, no Monet scratching at the screen, no wind stirring the trees, no traffic noise.

Kiki pulled on the screen door and pushed the inner door open with her foot. "Gabrielle!" She entered. "Gabrielle!" She walked through the kitchen and straight to the phone. The receiver was dangling in midair. As she replaced it on the hook she heard a noise—a moaning sound. Andrew looked at her, and the two teenagers quickly made their way to the bedroom.

Monet was on a blanket on the floor, whimpering softly. There was a strange odor in the room.

"What stinks?" Andrew asked.

"I think someone's chloroformed him," Kiki said, getting down beside the big dog. "He's whimpering in his sleep."

"Well, Gabrielle's not in the house," Andrew said. "I'm going to check the van."

He was back in a few minutes. "Not there, and not in the toolshed, either. Doesn't look like anything's been disturbed."

"I think we should check the barn," Kiki

said, thinking about Dr. Allenby's comment to her mother. She got up and started for the door.

"Monet?" Andrew asked.

"I think he'll be all right," she said. "His breathing is strong. I think he'll just have to sleep it off."

The big main doors on the barn wouldn't open, so Kiki and Andrew walked around the building until they found a side door. They left it open as they entered; the light inside was minimal and came mostly from cracks in the arched roof, above the hayloft.

"Gabrielle!" Kiki yelled as she walked in. She moved to a stall that was neatly covered with a large sheet of plastic. Dust flew in all directions as she lifted the the covering. Underneath were a dozen ornately framed paintings—most were pastoral scenes, some as big as the museum pieces at the Galliard. The next stall had portraits, and the third contained a rack of unframed canvases. On the opposite wall were shelves filled with pottery and small statuary. Kiki picked up a cobalt-blue fluted bowl and turned it over. On the bottom were the initials *G. J.* in a stylish script. *Gabrielle Janssen*. But where was she?

Kiki's eyes misted over. She walked to the side door and stepped out into the sunshine.

"Andrew," she said as they took the path back to the house, "they wouldn't kill her until they have the Galliard artifacts, would they?"

"It wouldn't make any sense if they did," he replied. "Maybe we should just call the police and tell them what's happening."

"But they'd arrest Gabrielle!" Kiki said. "There's got to be another way! I'll think of something. And besides, we can't tell them what's happening, because we don't really know. If we accuse Van Kayser of kidnapping, and then find out she really has gone to Pennsylvania and Monet's just been given some medicine by the vet . . ."

She looked in again on the sleeping dog, and Andrew filled his water dish before they got on their bikes for the ride back.

"He's got plenty of food," Andrew said. "I guess if I'd been shot and chloroformed in the last three days I wouldn't be hungry, either. It sort of dulls the appetite."

They made the long ride back without much conversation, but when they were within four blocks of Kiki's house, she suddenly braked to a stop. "You know what?" she said excitedly. "Gabrielle herself doesn't know where the artifacts are! She can't tell Van Kayser where to find them, even to save her own life! We're the ones who hid them when we took them from the toolshed. Did you say anything to her about it?"

Andrew shook his head. "I couldn't. Dr. Locker was there. And we were all too worried about Monet. I didn't even think about telling her." He grinned at Kiki and pushed his hair back off his forehead. "Actually, Dr. Van Kayser," he said in an affected voice, "you will find the crown jewels in the dog-food bag, and the Ming vase in the clothes hamper, and the—"

"Let's go!" Kiki yelled. When she reached the house she dashed inside and grabbed the kitchen phone book. "Van Kayser . . . Van Kayser . . ." she muttered to herself. She closed the book and grimaced. "Not listed," she said.

"Try information," Andrew suggested. "Maybe his beach house listing is new." But the operator didn't have a listing, either.

"He called Elena from his beach house this morning," Kiki said. "So he has a phone out there. Well, I guess we'll pay a visit to our good friend. She'll have the number."

"Are you crazy? She's not going to give you anything but a headache," Andrew said.

"You're probably right. I'll have to think of a creative way to get the information."

"Like Chinese water torture?"

"No," said Kiki, grinning. "Something with more class."

Kiki and Andrew worked out the details of their plan while they were riding the bus to the museum. When they got off, they went in separately, as if they didn't know each other. Kiki hung around the marble staircase in the rotunda while Andrew approached the woman at the front desk.

"I'd like to see Elena Morgan," he said.

"Elena Morgan," the receptionist repeated, consulting a list.

"She's an intern in the curator's office."

"Oh, yes. I see her name here. It's hard to keep all these people straight. And I'm only here two days a month. We're all volunteers, you know. Keeps expenses down." She dialed a number and waited.

"There's a gentleman at the desk to see you, Ms. Morgan," she said. "Shall I send him up?"

Kiki could see Andrew shaking his head and giving the receptionist a frantic look as she asked Elena the question.

The receptionist looked up and covered the mouthpiece with her hand.

"Ah . . . we already arranged it," he whispered, just loud enough for Kiki to hear. "I'll meet her in the cafeteria."

The woman removed her hand. "Excuse

me, Ms. Morgan, what was that? . . . I see."
She looked up again. "What is your name,
young man?"

Kiki could see the back of Andrew's neck
getting red.

"Uh, Troy."

The receptionist repeated the name and
added, "He'd like to meet you in the cafeteria."

She hung up the phone. "She'll be right
down," she said. "But I'm not sure they're still
serving in the cafeteria. It's almost closing
time." She turned to take an incoming call.

Kiki gave Andrew a thumbs-up signal and
ran up the stairs, while Andrew quickly
walked from the rotunda to the end of the
hallway and the staircase that led to the basement.

When Kiki got to the third floor, she
glanced at the light panel above the elevator.
It was at the second floor and descending. By
now, Andrew should be safely out of sight in
the restoration studio. She was trusting to
luck that, in her haste to see Troy, Elena had
left the curator's door unlocked. Kiki walked
cautiously down the hall and put her hand on
the knob. It turned easily. She shut the door
behind her and went straight to the desk, sit-

ting down in Van Kayser's big leather swivel chair.

An address file of small cards on a rotary wheel was in the first drawer she opened. She flipped the cards to the *V*'s. Vabille. Vacca. Vassier. No Van Kayser. *Would he even keep his own phone number in a card file?* Kiki wondered. *Probably not under his surname.* She looked in the *L*'s. Lansden. Larry. Lillian. Lolbrecht. No Ludwig.

Try location. D's. David. Deer Lake Service Station. Close! Her heart was pounding. Dougherty. Dresler. She shuffled through the whole *D* section again. There was nothing that came closer to a Deer Lake beach house. *Beach house?* She tried the *B*'s with no success.

Kiki put the file back in the drawer and closed it, glancing nervously at the door. She wasn't sure how long Elena would wait in the cafeteria for the mythical Troy. And it was close to closing time. Would Elena come back upstairs or just leave? No, she'd come back up. She hadn't even locked the office door.

Kiki scooted the chair back a little to open the middle drawer. Pens, pencils, some antacid tablets, and some loose change. She was about to try the drawer to the right when she saw a telephone-message slip with one edge tucked under the desk blotter. *Elena—In an emergency, I can be reached at 555-6363. LVK.*

Success! Kiki slipped the note in her pocket and left, reaching the top of the stairs just as the elevator doors opened. As they did the museum's closing-time buzzer sounded. She ran down the three flights to the basement, where Andrew was waiting—not too patiently—in the studio.

"Got it!" she said, waving the pink telephone note. "As soon as everyone clears out, we'll go up and make a call."

"Calls, plural," Andrew said. "I have to check in or my mother will send out a search party. And if I get to a phone before five-thirty, I can talk to our pleasant, impersonal, no-questions-asked answering machine." He looked at Kiki. "Come to think of it, what are you doing here? You're grounded."

"I know. I guess I'll have to make a call, too, and just take my chances."

"How come Gabrielle doesn't have a phone down here?"

"Van Kayser said it would cost too much to put one in."

"Cheapskate."

"Won't we run into custodians upstairs?" Andrew asked.

"No, the museum uses a cleaning service. They come in the early morning."

They waited until five-twenty-five, munching on some stale soda crackers that Gabrielle had on a shelf. Andrew checked his watch. "I'm running out of friendly-answering-machine time," he said. "Do you think it's safe up there?"

Kiki nodded. "They all should be gone by now."

In the fading light of day, the rotunda of the museum, now empty of people, looked larger and more stately, like a cathedral or a state capitol building.

"We can use the phone at the front desk," Kiki whispered, "if we sit on the floor behind the desk. Otherwise, we might be seen from the street. There's a lot of traffic out there."

"They'd have to have awfully good eyes to see inside a building set this far back, at this time of day, going thirty-five miles an hour," Andrew groused. Then he grinned at her. "Okay, I'll stay out of sight." He dialed his home number.

"Good evening, mater and pater," he said in a false French accent. "Thees ees your loving son Andrew, to tell you I am going to get zee hamburgaire and shake and take in a flick at zee cinema. I weel not be late! Adios!"

He hung up the receiver and blew his breath out through his mouth. "Whew! Made it!"

"Me next," said Kiki, reaching for the phone. "It's me, Mom," she said when the recorder clicked in. "I'm at the museum still. Something came up that had to be taken care of tonight. I'll explain when I get home." She replaced the receiver and looked at Andrew. "She is going to be ticked off," she said, "but I don't know what else to tell her."

"You mean you are in deep doo-doo," he said.

Kiki nodded. "Understatement."

Daylight was fading quickly. "We need a flashlight," Kiki said. "I didn't know it would be this dark in here. There's one downstairs on the workbench."

Andrew loped off down the hall while Kiki sat hunched over behind the reception desk, worrying—about Gabrielle's safety, about Monet, about her mother's reaction to her not coming home after work, and about the plan that she and Andrew were about to put into motion. She was so deep in worrisome thought that when she felt the thump on her back, instead of whirling around or yelling out, she just froze, like a statue. Her heart was beating so loudly she could hear it in her ears as she slowly turned around.

Meeeooow!

"Pumpkin!" This time she did yell, and Andrew came running up the stairs waving the flashlight.

"Where'd he come from?" he asked.

Kiki shrugged. "I have no idea. I haven't seen him since he attacked Mr. Blondell's poodle last night." She pulled the big furry orange cat up across her knees and hugged him. "But I'm glad you're here," she said.

Pumpkin purred his response.

"Okay," Andrew said, "next on the plan is a call to Van Kayser, right?"

"Right. Hold the flashlight over here so I can read this number." She smoothed out the slip of paper she'd taken from the curator's desk and dialed. "Wish me luck."

"Do you think he'll recognize your voice?"

"He only talked to me a couple of times. I don't think so."

Kiki listened as the phone rang. On the third ring, a man answered.

"Dr. Van Kayser, please," she said.

There was a pause.

"Dr. Van Kayser, this is Betty in the New York office of Stottmeier and Dresler. Mr. Dresler asked me to give you a message . . . Yes, it is late here. I'm working overtime. He said it was important . . . Well, I had trouble getting a number where I could reach you . . . From your secretary, Miss Morgan . . . Yes, well, the message is that Mr. Dresler wants you and Janssen to meet him at the museum tonight at ten past nine. He said to tell you he knows where the missing goods are. Oh, and he also asked me to remind you that he has a buyer coming into New York tomorrow for the cat and that he's counting on you to make that important phone call at nine." Andrew rolled his eyes and made a face at her that almost started her laughing. "Dr. Van Kayser," she continued sweetly, "I certainly hope you understand what all that means, because I don't."

Pumpkin had sat up straight and pointed his ears when he heard the word *cat*, and Andrew stroked his back.

Kiki took the receiver from her ear, looked at it, and slammed it down on the phone. "Rude old scuzzball," she said.

"What did he say?" Andrew asked.

"When I said that I didn't understand what it meant, he said I wasn't supposed to and hung up in my ear."

"Do you think he'll show up?"

"I figure he has to. If he thinks Dresler

knows where the Galliard artifacts are, he's going to be here. Dresler could take off with them. No honor among thieves."

"Good thing you knew about the buyer coming into New York tomorrow, and using Elena's name was good. He can't think it's a hoax when he hears facts like that!"

Kiki nodded. "I hope Gabrielle's all right," she said.

"Say, how does the security system inside work?" Andrew asked, pulling Pumpkin back by his tail as he tried to run off. "I mean, Gabrielle explained about the door alarms, but what about the exhibits? If Pumpkin runs around, is he going to set one off?"

"Probably. He did the other night," Kiki answered. "There's not a video system or anything like that. But I think all the exhibit rooms have motion detectors. We're okay in the halls. Let's take him down to the studio. Otherwise he'll be attacking every forgery in the building!"

"Come on, Kiki, you don't really believe that, do you?" Andrew asked as they went downstairs.

"Yes, I really do!" Kiki snapped. "He has some kind of a sensor of his own. He did it with the Yuan-dynasty vase and the Pueblo jar."

"And don't forget the carob chip cookies at the Kendricks'!" Andrew said. "Come to think of it, Betty, he should have been after you upstairs when you were faking your identity!"

Kiki's irritation turned to giggles. "That's different, Troy," she replied. "I'd like to know how he got here, but that's another unsolved Pumpkin mystery. Maybe he was here all day."

"Nah," said Andrew. "He would have attacked Elena if he'd been here that long."

"You're probably right," said Kiki.

She pushed open the door to the restoration lab and they went inside and sat on the floor to wait.

Chapter Twelve

The three-hour wait went by more quickly than either one had expected. They went over their plan several times, arguing about some of the details, agreeing on others, and discarding some entirely. And this time Kiki had remembered to pick up a deck of cards when they'd stopped at her house to leave their bikes.

At ten to nine Andrew stood up and stretched. "It's time," he said.

Kiki nodded. She picked up Pumpkin and opened the studio door. "Bring the flashlight," she said. She walked down the basement hall in the opposite direction from the stairs. "The window's down here," she said, turning the corner.

At the end of the hallway, at ceiling height, was a small oblong slit. Inside, the glass was dirty. Outside, iron bars protected against unlawful entrance. "It looks out on the parking lot," Kiki explained. "We're just to the right of the loading dock. Can you see anything?"

Andrew stretched up to look. "It would be easier if I'd spent the day on a rack," he said, grinning. "I need to be about six inches taller. I'm going back to get a box. There were some crates in the hall by the studio."

"I'll get one," Kiki said. "Give me the flashlight. You keep watching." She turned and went back down the hallway, carrying Pumpkin in one arm and the flashlight in the other hand.

"How am I going to do this?" she muttered to herself, training the flashlight on the stack of crates. "That one looks about right."

The box she was looking at was underneath two others. It was solid wood, not just slatted like the others, about eight inches high, and had a sturdy, hinged cover. She boosted Pumpkin up to her shoulder with a terse "Stay there!" and set the flashlight down on the floor. But Pumpkin, in his usual autocratic manner, had no intention of staying on Kiki's shoulder. He jumped off, expertly avoiding her quick grab at him, circled around once, and ran up the stairs.

Kiki stood and stared, weighing the consequences of going after him. If he ventured out of the rotunda and into one of the exhibit rooms, he might set off an alarm, ruining the entire plan. If she went after him, she was likely to do the same thing herself. Well, now they'd all have to take their chances!

She wrenched the box from the pile and carried it back to Andrew, who was still standing on tiptoe with his nose resting on the window ledge.

"Here," she said, setting the box down. "Pumpkin's gone. He's somewhere upstairs. I was so dumb! I should have left him with you. We planned everything else so carefully, and now that crazy cat is running around up there." She knew the tension in her voice was obvious. She was close to tears.

"Quit beating yourself up," Andrew said, trying to cheer her up. He climbed on the box. "Nothing you can do about it now. It took him a few minutes to trip the alarm last time, so I bet those sensors are set to pick up movement at a height of four or five feet. Like for a human being walking upright. As long as he stays at floor level, nothing will happen."

She felt a little better. Andrew was always so much calmer than she was when things went wrong. "Have you ever known my great leaping Leo to stay at floor level for more than two minutes?" she said wryly, climbing up on the box beside Andrew just in time to see the

167

lights of a vehicle sweep across the parking lot.

"Here comes somebody!" Andrew said excitedly.

"That's not Van Kayser's car. It must be Dresler." They watched two people get out of the car. The driver took a long box from the trunk, and they walked toward the building, disappearing from sight as they reached the ramp to the loading dock.

"That's the fake ebony cat, I bet," Kiki whispered. "The box is about the right size."

"At least they're coming in the right order," Andrew said. "If Van Kayser and Gabrielle had come early, we'd be in big trouble."

They waited in silence for a short while, then Kiki said, "They must be inside now. I wish we could hear something."

Andrew checked his watch. "Judging from our time the other night, they can make it up to the second floor in about two and a half minutes. They're probably in the Egyptian room by now."

"And here comes Van Kayser," Kiki said, straining to see through the barred window. "Gabrielle's with him!" She watched as the curator walked from the driver's side to the passenger's, and unlocked the door. "Gabrielle's okay!"

"If you call having a gun in your back okay," Andrew muttered. Van Kayser was staying close behind Gabrielle, holding something up against her back.

"This is where the timing gets tricky," Andrew said, stepping off the box. "Let's go!"

The two teenagers ran up the stairs and across the rotunda to the reception desk. They sat on the floor and Kiki pulled the phone down into her lap. Andrew held the flashlight low on the numbers as she dialed 911.

"There's a robbery in progress at the Galliard Museum," she whispered into the mouthpiece.

"Your name, please."

"Kiki Collier."

Footsteps! Van Kayser and Gabrielle were approaching the rotunda from the back hall.

"I'm checking our alert system, Ms. Collier." There was a brief pause. "The Galliard has been cleared for after-hours entry." The operator's voice sounded very loud to Kiki.

"But—" Kiki had her mouth on the phone and was whispering.

"We show that the curator called at eight-fifty-nine. Thank you for your concern."

Kiki put down the receiver. Gabrielle and Van Kayser were in the rotunda and approaching the stairs. She looked at Andrew in dismay.

"Authorized after-hours entry," she whispered. "They're not coming."

"We've lost our chance," Andrew said. "They're on their way up."

"Give me some light!" Kiki picked up the receiver and dialed another number.

Mrs. Kendrick's familiar, cheerful voice came on the line almost immediately.

"Mrs. Kendrick, this is Kiki," she whispered. "Is Mr. Kendrick home?"

"Just a minute, I'll get him."

"No!" Kiki said. "I don't have time to explain. I'm at the museum. Just tell him to come quick and bring the police. I already called 911 and they say it's an authorized entry, but there's a robbery going on here right now!"

Mrs. Kendrick gasped. "I'll tell him. Be careful, Kiki!" she said.

"Let's go!" Kiki said to Andrew, and the two of them charged across the rotunda to the curving staircase. They took the stairs two at a time, slowed as they approached the Egyptian collection, and stopped just outside the arch.

Voices, angry voices, came from the room. Kiki peered in and motioned to Andrew.

"They're over by the case with the *udjat* eye jewelry." They crept into the room, crouching down so they wouldn't be seen, and ducked behind the sarcophagus. Van Kayser still had Gabrielle in front of him, and the other two, a man and a woman, were facing them. Even in the dim light, Kiki could see a long scratch from temple to chin on Gabrielle's face.

"So you're here to check up on me!" Dresler said.

"I'm here because your New York secretary called and told me to be here, and to bring Janssen. She said you have the goods."

"You're making it up! I didn't tell my secretary to call! And what goods are you talking about?"

"It was Betty or Patty or something. And I assumed she meant the Galliard pieces."

"My New York secretary is Annamarie," said Dresler slowly. "I don't believe you! And furthermore, Ludwig, this key your intern gave me is useless!" He threw the key on the floor.

"What are you talking about?" Van Kayser asked, stooping to pick it up. As he did there was a loud crash.

Kiki jumped, and Van Kayser whirled around. The ebony cat was lying on the floor three feet from its pedestal, and regally posed in its place was Pumpkin!

"Gabrielle, run!" Kiki shouted.

An orange streak flashed by and leaped to the top of the jewelry case, hissing. Gabrielle headed for the stairs, closely followed by Andrew and Kiki.

"Shoot that animal!" Van Kayser shouted.

A shot rang out, and there was a screech. Kiki spun around and ran back into the room. "Pumpkin!" she yelled.

But Van Kayser's shot had missed its mark. Kiki could see the cat's green eyes glowing as he poised himself on top of the sarcophagus, ready to spring again. There was a noise behind her, and someone grabbed her around the neck. Dresler!

"Pumpkin!" she yelled again, and the big cat leaped from the concrete crypt to Dresler's back, digging his claws into the back of his head and biting his neck. Dresler screamed and let go of Kiki. Pumpkin lunged from the man's back at Van Kayser's hand, knocking the gun to the marble floor, where it skittered away under a display case. The woman with Dresler, who had ducked down behind a display case, grabbed the crate they had brought in with them and headed for the doorway.

Kiki ran past her with the curator in pursuit and Pumpkin close behind.

"I've wanted to do this since Monday," Kiki mumbled to herself as she flung a leg over the banister and rode it to the first floor, leaving Pumpkin chasing Van Kayser down the stairs. The wily cat got ahead of the curator by a step, and that was all that was needed. Van Kayser tripped and fell the last ten steps and landed, stunned, at the bottom of the staircase.

Outside the glass doors of the museum, Kiki could see the flashing red lights of police vehicles. From the delivery entrance, Andrew and Gabrielle were ushering three officers into the rotunda. Close behind them was Mr. Kendrick, dressed in an old sweatshirt and tennis shoes.

"Kiki! Are you all right?" he asked, hurrying to her side.

"I'm okay," she said. "There are two others upstairs in the Egyptian room."

Two of the officers took the stairs on the run, but before they reached the top there were sounds of a scuffle from above, and a man and a cat yowled at the same time.

"I'd know that voice anywhere," Mr. Kendrick said, hugging Kiki.

"I guess he went back up to finish the job,"

she said, leaning up against him. "Thanks for coming."

"Glad I was able to," Mr. Kendrick said. "Can we sit down somewhere and sort all this out? The officers will take care of the suspects."

Kiki nodded.

"Nice to see you again, Mrs. Janssen," Mr. Kendrick said, reaching across and shaking Gabrielle's hand. "We're both dressed a little differently than we were on Wednesday night!" Gabrielle was in her usual coveralls. "Hi, Andrew!" He slapped Andrew on the shoulder and grinned. "Now, where can we talk?"

Gabrielle led the way to the cafeteria and turned on the lights.

"Who wants to start?" Mr. Kendrick asked as they seated themselves at a table.

"I will talk," Gabrielle said. She looked very pale and tired, and Kiki wondered if she'd slept at all the night before.

All three of them took turns talking. They told Mr. Kendrick the whole story—about Van Kayser's thefts from the museum, the break-in at Gabrielle's home, the search of her studio and the shooting of Monet, and finally her kidnapping in order to force her to tell where the treasures were. When she admitted to taking the artifacts and making reproductions, both Kiki and Andrew interrupted in her defense and had to be shushed by Mr. Kendrick so Gabrielle could finish.

"It seems to me that there are extenuating circumstances for your illegal acts, Mrs. Janssen," he said, pushing his glasses up on his head and rubbing his eyes. "It will be up to the Galliard board to decide whether or not charges will be filed. I'm sure that right now the police are running ID checks on Van Kayser and his friends. Interpol should have something on his record as Stottmeier. There won't be any problem with you going home." He stood up. "But you'll all have to go down to the police station to give your statements first."

"I need to call my mother first," Kiki said. "She's going to be furious. And I need to find Pumpkin."

Mr. Kendrick smiled. "I'll call your mother," he said. "And Susan. She was worried about you. You go and find Pumpkin." They turned the lights out in the cafeteria, and Andrew showed Mr. Kendrick where the front desk phone was. The rotunda lights were on now, and a uniformed policeman was standing guard at the front entrance.

"Have you seen a big orange cat?" Kiki asked him.

"Yes, ma'am," he said. "And the skinny black one, too. They checked me out about fifteen minutes ago, went into that room over there, and haven't come out." He pointed toward the American Indian exhibit room.

"Skinny black one?" Kiki repeated. Her heart was thumping in her throat.

"That's right, miss. Following right along behind! Like the big orange one was giving it a tour of the place!"

"Thanks," Kiki said. A shiver ran up her spine, and she jumped when Andrew came up behind her.

"You look like you've seen a ghost," he kidded.

"Heard about one," she said.

"Where's Pumpkin?"

"He's after the Pueblo jar again." She looked questioningly at the officer. "Have you heard any crashes?"

"Nope."

Kiki walked toward the exhibit room with Andrew and Gabrielle following. When she got to the doorway, she slowed her pace and advanced quietly toward the pedestal that held the earthenware jar. She stopped. Pumpkin was clearly silhouetted in the dim light that came from the rotunda. He was sitting regally on his haunches, tail swept around in front to cover his feet, neck arched and head held high. And he was right in front of the pedestal, gazing up at the Pueblo jar. There was no black cat in sight. The policeman must have been kidding her. Someone must have told him about the ebony cat upstairs.

"Well, so much for the cat-that-can-fake-out-a-forgery theory," Andrew teased. "He should have had that thing in smithereens fifteen minutes ago." He looked over at Kiki. "But he's still an exceptional cat," he added.

"I don't understand it," Kiki said. "He knew every other piece that was a fake. Even tonight, when he toppled the ebony cat. He knew that they'd already exchanged it."

"But the Pueblo jar is not a forgery." Gabrielle spoke quietly.

"But . . ." Kiki turned around and stared at her. "But the real jar was in your toolshed. We saw it!"

"Saw it?" Andrew hooted. "We hid it! I personally put it in Monet's dog-food bag—that big forty-pound job behind the kitchen door."

"Yes," said Gabrielle, "but I took it out."

Mr. Kendrick walked into the room and stood quietly behind her, listening.

"And I also found the objects in the clothes

hamper, and under the bed, and in the wastebasket . . ." There was a smile in her voice as she listed the places in which Kiki and Andrew had hidden things. "But the best one of all, I think, was the oil painting in the bathtub!"

"You found them all?" Kiki asked, wide-eyed.

"Yes," said Gabrielle. "I found them and I returned them. They are all back in place here in the museum. You see, I came back yesterday afternoon after I had checked on Monet. I could not bear the weight of the deceit any longer."

"I knew someone had been in the studio!" Kiki said. "But I didn't think it was you."

"Yes, it was I."

Andrew looked at Kiki and let out a long breath. "I guess it's a good thing that our original plan got messed up," he said.

Gabrielle looked perplexed, and Mr. Kendrick stepped up beside her. "It seems that there's more to be told here," he said dryly. "What, pray tell, was your original plan?"

"Originally, we thought that we could stop Van Kayser and Gabrielle as they came in tonight and strike a deal with him."

"A deal?" Mr. Kendrick shouted in a horrified voice.

"Well," Andrew explained, "we didn't think Gabrielle knew where we'd hidden the artifacts." He was touching the tips of his fingers together, and Kiki knew he was nervous. "We were going to tell him that she really didn't know where they were anymore, because we were the ones who had hidden them, and that if he'd let her go downstairs to her studio, we'd go out to her farm with him and get him the things he wanted."

"That way," Kiki cut in, "Gabrielle would have been safe downstairs, and the pair upstairs wouldn't even have known she was here. The police would have come and caught Dresler and his partner, and then Gabrielle would have come upstairs and told them that we were on the way to her farm with Van Kayser. So the three of us would end up safe, and the three of them would be in custody."

"But it all got messed up," Andrew continued, "when the 911 operator wouldn't send the police. We couldn't stop Van Kayser in the rotunda until we knew that the police were coming."

"That's when I called you," Kiki said.

"That's quite a plan," said Mr. Kendrick, with both admiration and irritation in his voice. "You two do have ingenious minds!" He stared at the two teenagers. "But don't ever ever try to make a deal with a crook again. You've been lucky, but you can't trust people who work outside the law. You never know what they'll do. Okay?"

Andrew and Kiki exchanged looks. "Okay," said Andrew.

Kiki went over to Pumpkin and knelt down beside him. He was purring softly and still staring at the Indian bowl. "Come on, Pumpkin," she said softly, gathering the big cat up in her arms. "We're going to go now." She looked at Mr. Kendrick. "What did my mother say?"

"Things are okay with your mom," he said, smiling at her. "She's going to call your mother, too, Andrew, and explain what's happened. Then she's coming down to meet us at the police station."

"Thanks," said Kiki, obviously relieved. "I was worried about that."

"Me, too," said Andrew.

Mr. Kendrick hooted. "I don't believe it! You two kids think nothing of taking on three armed art thieves, and your biggest worry is your mothers! It's great! I love it!"

"Don't forget that we had Pumpkin, too," Kiki said, rubbing her cheek up against the cat's soft fur. "If he hadn't knocked the gun out of Van Kayser's hand, this might have had a different ending."

"Speaking of guns," Gabrielle said, "would you happen to know how one got into the vegetable bin in my refrigerator?"

"Oh, that was Pumpkin's doing, too!" Kiki said. "Well, Andrew actually put it there, after he threw the orange that knocked it out of the man's hand. Andrew took it off the piano because that was Pumpkin territory."

"I don't believe this," said Mr. Kendrick, holding his head as they walked to his car out in front.

Gabrielle chuckled. "Pumpkin has an affinity for guns and an aversion to forged art objects. What talent!"

"There's just one other thing," Kiki said, turning to Mr. Kendrick. He held the front door open for her as Andrew and Gabrielle climbed into the back seat.

"What's that?"

She fished her keychain out of her pocket and removed one of the keys. "This is the key to the *udjat* eye jewelry case," she said, handing it to him. "Van Kayser has the key to my bicycle lock. I'll trade with him . . . before Monday. I'll need it for school."

"Sorry, Kiki. I'll buy you a new lock. The

key to your bike lock is going to be state's evidence." He started the motor and steered slowly around the curving driveway in front of the museum. Then, without warning, he hit the brakes.

"I'll be a—!" He let out a deep breath. "Where did she come from?"

Sitting on the hood of his car was a lean, glossy, short-haired black cat.

"The ebony cat," Kiki whispered to herself as Pumpkin purred in her lap.

The cat sat as still as a statue, staring in at Kiki. She flicked her tail once, and with the grace of a ballerina jumped from the hood and disappeared into the bushes.

Mr. Kendrick shook his head and eased the car out into traffic.

No one spoke. Kiki felt Gabrielle's hand on her shoulder. Something slipped down into her lap. She looked down. It was the *udjat* eye ring on the black plaited cord.

"It is for you," Gabrielle said quietly.

"But—"

"But yes," Gabrielle said firmly. "To remind you of possibilities. And Kiki . . . thank you."

When Kiki and Andrew got to school Monday morning, they were celebrities. Every paper in the state had run a feature story about the teenagers who'd smashed the forgery ring. And almost every student in the school had some comment, except for Elena Morgan, who was noticeably quiet on the subject.

On Monday night, Mrs. Kendrick called Kiki.

"I thought you would like to know," she said, "that the Galliard Board of Trustees had an emergency meeting today. They've decided that no charges will be filed against Mrs. Janssen, since she was acting in the interests of the museum. In fact, we've asked her to serve as acting curator until another can be found. We offered her the curator's job on a permanent basis, but she declined."

"I'm glad nobody blames her. Thanks for letting me know."

"Kiki, is your mom home? May I speak to her?"

With a puzzled look, Kiki handed the phone to Dr. Collier and leaned her elbows on the counter, chin in hands, to listen. She didn't learn much from her mother's side of the conversation.

"Yes, early June would be fine. That's wonderful! It will be good for her and good for us. Thanks, Susan. Bye."

"What was that all about?" Kiki asked.

Dr. Collier smiled. "Don't be nosy," she said, teasing. "You don't tell *me* everything—obviously," she added pointedly. She started ticking things off on her fingers. "Art thieves, kidnappings, dogs with gunshot wounds, forgeries . . ."

"Come on, Mom! What are you and Mrs. Kendrick cooking up?"

"You'll like it," her mother said. "Gabrielle Janssen is going to put on a one-woman show in early June in the hospital auditorium."

"All that stuff she has in the barn?" Kiki said.

Dr. Collier nodded. "She agreed to do it on the basis that half of the proceeds of what she sells will go to the children's wing at the hospital."

"That's super! Wait till I tell Andrew!"

Kiki picked up the phone and dialed Carlisles' number from memory while Pumpkin stretched his long body and let out a resounding meow.

EXCITING MYSTERIES!

**Meet Kiki and her cat Pumpkin...Together
they share a special talent—for solving crimes!**

Kiki's pretty busy these days...writing for the school paper,
cooking dinner to help out her mom, and playing tennis with
her friend Andrew. But she still finds time to tackle some local
mysteries, with the help of her cat Pumpkin (named for the
color of his fur). Pumpkin's a big fan of chocolate, riding in
Kiki's back pack, and using his uncanny sense for mystery to
help Kiki solve crimes—and stay out of danger!

___**"THIEF!" SAID THE CAT**   0-425-12732-X/$3.50
  By Louise Munro Foley
There's a break-in while Kiki's babysitting! Pumpkin manages to
scare the burglars away, but not before they've left behind some
very interesting clues...

___**"BLOOD!" SAID THE CAT**   0-425-12655-2/$3.50
Kiki discovers more at the local museum than she'd ever expected,
including an art-theft scheme! She's counting on Pumpkin to keep
track of the priceless treasures, while she tracks down the culprits.

Coming in September '92
___**"POISON!" SAID THE CAT**   0-425-12898-9/$3.50
Students at Pioneer Junior High are getting sick from food
poisoning...but is someone doing it on purpose? Kiki and Pumpkin
uncover an unlikely villain behind a sinister plot.

GET READY FOR ABIGAIL, MELISSA, AND JULIA AND THEIR OUTRAGEOUS SCHEMES FOR SUCCESS!

Abigail just has to have a leather jacket. Julia needs new clothes, and Melissa dreams of writing books on a computer. But Abigail and her friends are broke until they decide to form The 3 p.m. Club and start up their first business!

__**THE 3 P.M. CLUB #1: GET RICH QUICK! (OR TIE-DYE TRYING)**
by Leslie McGuire $3.50/0-425-12968-3 (June)
What a great way to start a business—making tie-dye T-shirts. The T-shirts are a hit, but when Melissa's brother Walt gets into the picture, disaster strikes! Abigail has a major crush on Walt, but will the 3 p.m. Club's first business go out of business before he notices her? Can the girls turn things around before it's too late?

__**THE 3 P.M. CLUB #2: MY HAIR TURNED GREEN (I FEEL BLUE)**
by Leslie McGuire $3.50/0-425-12653 (August)
With their All Natural Beauty Salon, the girls can help the environment and make a little money, too. Besides, Melissa's determined to give herself a perm (her brother's friend, John, likes curly hair). But when Melissa's hair turns green the girls realize maybe they're in the wrong business.